Vinland Viking

A Saga

Gary L. Doman, M.A.

PublishAmerica
Baltimore

First printing

ISBN: 1-4137-6377-4
PUBLISHED BY PUBLISHAMERICA, LLLP
www.publishamerica.com
Baltimore

Printed in the United States of America

My thanks to John Sarsgard for his photography; thanks also to Rick Shaefer and Ed Cook, both of whom, when I flinched at the thought of having to do all the work necessary to write this book, told me that the idea is so good that it would be unethical not to publish it.

In the Year of Our Lord 1000, Yngar Magnusson stood aboard an Icelandic vessel sailing for the New World. With detachment he surveyed the polar horizon; the hues of the land- and seascape nearly matched those of his steel-colored eyes and light brownish gray follicles, mustache, and beard (also distinguishing the appearance of this 19-year-old was his ample musculature and height of 73 inches). What engrossed him much more than did his surroundings was reflecting on his erstwhile effort to escape the impact of Christianity, which had largely replaced worship of the more traditional Nordic deities. Like a hound on the trail of its quarry, the new faith seemed to have pursued him relentlessly, from his birth in the Orkney Islands on the site of Maeshowe to Iceland (where, just this year, it had become officially established); it was even infecting his ancestral homeland, Norway. His late parents had secured his baptism, but had then sent him to be raised by a foster father (that being a common practice among Scandians) whom they respected but didn't know to be a pagan; that episode had been his lone respite from the intrusive beliefs, but the foster father, too, was now dead. Keeping his religious freedom, he mused, no matter how many times he had to move in order to do so, had definitely become the theme of his life.

He hoped that, as one among the first shipload of settlers to be transported to the incipient Vinland colony (named Hvitramannaland, literally "white-men's land," after a country said in an Icelandic version of a medieval European legend to lie a six-days' sail west of Ireland; an alternate name for the new territory was Greater Ireland), he would finally be free to practice Asatru, devotion to the Old Gods (in particular, Thor, whose status as the favorite of the people aided his cult in persisting while the rest of the Norse pantheon humiliatingly surrendered to Yahwe). He even expected this, for was not the founder of this settlement, Leif Ericsson, the son of the notorious heathen Eric the Red? Surely he would be loyal to the ways of his sire.

As it turned out, Yngar (a native speaker of our tongue would Anglicize the Old Norse pronunciation of his name by voicing the "Y" as in "lynx" and the second syllable as the first in "garfish") would be as disappointed in this respect as in all others. The ship anchored near the site of the future town of Argentia, on Placentia Bay on the southwest coast of Newfoundland's

Avalon Peninsula, and organizing of the colony was carried out. Most of the inhabitants would earn a living by fishing or lumbering or, as Yngar intended, entering the highly profitable trade in walrus hides and ivory, and in gyrfalcons, from the Arctic (perhaps he would even acquire a few narwhal tusks to be sold to European apothecaries as "alicorns" or unicorn horns, but probably not, for his upbringing inclined him to resist the temptation toward dishonesty); elements of civilization were introduced, including domestic animals such as elkhounds, torvmosehunds (swamp dogs), bear-dogs, skogkatts (Norwegian forest cats), and Icelandic ponies, as well as, more importantly, women. Not long afterward, though, Ericsson, considered the natural leader of the settlement because of his exploration of this land, made a fateful proclamation: he would accept the offer that some influential men had made him, and become the first Jarl (Earl) of Hvitramannaland. Yngar resented this decision not merely because he had come from the frontier society of Iceland, which prided itself on its independence and saw no need for a monarchy, but especially on account of the reason Jarl Leif stated for his governance: strong, central leadership apparently was needed to enforce universal conversion to Christianity.

The development dumbfounded Yngar and many others. None of them had known that Leif's (at least nominal) overlord, King Olav Tryggvesson of Norway, had earlier summoned the renowned explorer to his court and recommended that he adopt the new faith, and that Ericsson had subsequently become a great Christian proselytizer, persuading his people by warning that the first millennium since the birth of Christ would soon be upon them.

Though stunned, however, Yngar vowed not to submit. He wore a wolfscross, a combination of the crucifix and of Thor's famous war hammer Mjollnir; this symbol was employed by many other Norsemen during the adoption of Christianity, but for Yngar it was not a means of bridging the gap between the two religions but rather a way of protesting the new beliefs. He covertly inspired other recalcitrant young men to form with him a cabal of paganism; they rendered homage to the god of thunder in the deep of the woods which overspread their isle, or anywhere else they could find solitude. Yngar even located a woman who he knew to be a fellow believer and induced her to sew for them a raven standard, the very flag that his Viking forebears had carried into battle and flown above their watercrafts while plundering Christian communities. He knew of nowhere else to run; so be it, for he would run no more.

Yngar quickly came to desire to live more truly as a renegade, however, than he could by simply defying the new way of life in secret. He longed for the less-peaceful but electrifying days when the Northmen first became known abroad by going viking, that is, raiding the coastal cities and villages outside Scandinavia. To prove his armipotence in clashes with the finest warriors of other peoples, carry off slaves and other booty, and make the name Yngar Magnusson a source of terror to the kingdoms of his time: this it was for which he yearned.

Later that same year a drakkar, or dragon longship used only for war or for other reasons of state, came to Vinland with tidings whose very means of conveyance indicated that they must be of the greatest importance. King Olav Tryggvesson, who had led the struggle to establish Christianity in Norway and in the other regions (including Greater Ireland) claimed as possessions of his northern empire, who had fostered the development of the dragon ship, and who had become the subject of legends despite having reigned for just five years, was dead (Yngar's satisfaction at this report was offset by his learning that Eric the Red also had expired recently).

This was the first time that Yngar had actually seen one of the vessels that later people would forever associate with the Vikings he lionized. It required 60 rowers, whereas the craft in which he had come to this continent possessed only seven pairs of oars. His transportation, in fact, covered less area than did the 2,000-square-foot sail alone of the flagship, the total length of which stretched for over 113 feet. As the name "longship" implies, the timber leviathan was more modest in its other proportions, but its width still exceeded 17 feet and the sole mast (even without its surmounting weather vane) rose 57 feet toward heaven. The oars extended from its breadth, like the legs of an impossibly large, seagoing centipede, farther than would three tall men lying head-to-toe. For every oarsman there was a round Viking targe, 32 inches in diameter, perched vertically on the shield planks, or gunwales, of the hull's ornately decorated flanks; the iron boss at the center of each was aligned with the top rim of the ship's body, so that only the upper semicircles were visible to the rowers (who, when summoned to battle, would detach the shields and use them for personal defense). He calculated the approximate weight of the ash-wood hull to approach 15 tons; despite this bulk, the ship sat so delicately on the water (having a draft of merely a few feet) that it could travel up rivers too shallow for any other which normally plied the seas. The figurehead represented a dragon of fierce aspect, and it bore a corresponding tail at its stern; hence the designation for this class of vessel. Heathen

Northmen, in fact, considered such a ship not merely to resemble a living thing in some ways but even to be one, and this contributed to its mystique. As he stood on the shore of the harbor, gazing and gaping at the sight, the awe of the moment inspired in him a plan.

That night, while the royal drakkar rested at anchor, the local citizenry woke with alarm and rushed outside their homes; several knorrir, smaller ships used for trade, were aflame in the harbor. Leaders of the community immediately made preparations for dousing the blaze, and while they did so Yngar and his incendiary confederates boarded the dragon ship. They easily overcame the few sailors who had been left to guard it, but whose attention was focused on the fiery diversion, and hastily disposed of the awning that protected it from the elements when it lay in port.

Upon quenching the conflagration, the Christians saw that they had been duped, but it was too late to prevent the hijacked longship from leaving its anchorage; rather than bother to raise the sail, the recalcitrants had oared away as quickly as the strength of their arms would take them, guiding themselves with the illumination shed by the burning knorrir. They were still barely visible by the moonlight, though, and so the royal representatives manned the fastest ship of the Vinlanders and set off after them.

Once in the open ocean, the crew of the pirated drakkar unfurled their expansive sail so that they might save the power of their sinews for a hypothetical time when it would be necessary. King Olav's heralds proved dogged pursuers and worthy sailors, but Yngar, having gained nautical experience when living in the Orkneys and Iceland, had confidence that the handicap of an inferior vessel would damn their cause. The dragon ship indeed could travel at 14 knots, several knots more swiftly than could that of the King's men; the wind, though, originally favoring the renegades, began blowing opposite to the direction of both chased and chasing. This change in the weather meant that the parties would have to travel as nearly directly into the wind as possible, by tacking, that is to say, setting the sails at alternating 45-degree angles to the source of the gusts and thus zigzagging to the right, left, right, and so on. This was done. Yngar soon noticed with alarm that he could see occupants of the Norwegians' watercraft not previously visible to him; they were unmistakably closing the gap. He had no preparation for this development. I suppose it makes sense, he now thought grimly, that they're better at tacking simply because their vessel is smaller. He took a gamble: "Haul down the sail as quickly as you can, men, and set to rowing. It's the only way we can outrun them."

Many of the crew who hadn't observed the progress of the ship on their trail silently questioned his decision, but no one had the time to protest, for all knew as well as he that to fulfill his order would be a lengthy chore. After the commencement of the task the work proceeded so slowly that Yngar began to fear they would not in fact complete it soon enough to escape.

The drakkar had now lost so much of its lead as to be within range of bow and arrow, Yngar knew, of the men aboard the pursuing ship; he prayed to his deity that they were not thus armed, for if they so were they would have the means to slaughter all his followers and himself without resistance.

What seemed a long time went by. Then the wind, which had been blowing so robustly, unexpectedly calmed to such a degree that the Norwegians' rally was temporarily thwarted. Yngar, anticipating a gust strong enough to compensate for this halcyon interval, and seeing that his underlings had all but completed their task, commanded that they abort the rest of the operation and "Row till you feel that your arms will never work again; once we've escaped, you'll have all the time you need for resting!"

The men did their best to oblige him, and Yngar personally relieved one oarsman for whom going on would have been too great a struggle. The wind's loss of vigor indeed proved momentary; the muscles of the renegades, however, showed themselves equal to its force. The dragon ship rapidly increased the distance between itself and that of the Christians until the latter was no longer visible. Frustrated, but at least knowing that they could have tried no harder than they had, the representatives of the monarchy plied the waves for a while longer and then conceded defeat. Yngar and his followers made known to Thor their gratitude for deliverance.

A fog now blanketed the ocean, as if to confirm that the chase had ended, for it would have been impossible anyway for anyone to spot a vessel on the horizon in this new condition. Finally, though, visibility improved, and in time Yngar and his crew sighted Markland ("border land"), known later as southern Labrador, past which Leif Ericsson had voyaged before setting foot on Vinland. Leif had dubbed the new territory thus for the reason that it marked the northern limit of forested land, but the name was apt in an added sense, for the Northmen's world was one of coasts; they regarded the inland areas of most continents as forbidding places home only to monsters, and so it was natural that they should imagine this as a division between civilization and a realm where one would be foolish to venture.

The men under Yngar's command had trepidations, therefore, when he directed that they should take refuge in an inlet that interrupted the coastline.

He won them to his point of view when he reminded them that they would have to find harbor very soon, anyway, in order to replenish their store of provisions, and predicted that in the fiord they would have a place of concealment from possible enemies.

Yngar and company passed through the littoral canyon and landed on a desolate beach. The chill of the air was augmented by the newly roaring wind. The fugitives could see no form of life other than themselves and a few birds. It certainly seemed outside credulity that this might be (near, or perhaps the very place of) the Wonderstrand of which others had spoken. Yngar, having heard tales not only of supernatural beings but also of American Indians, whom the Northmen had dubbed "skraelings" (wretchcs), looked cautiously in every direction. Here, on the threshold of a vast continent of mystery (indeed, at the edge of their universe), they would begin their attempt to live lives of glory.

Months later, in 1001, the people of Newfoundland and of older Nordic domains were taking to grumbling about the plague that had come upon them. The plague owed its origin not to bacteria, but assumed the form of Brand-Yngar Magnusson (as men by this time knew him, "Brand" being a byname applied because of his use of arson to seize the craft now under his rule) and the heathens allied with him. Brand-Yngar, irrespective of his youth the obvious choice to skipper their rogue vessel, had personally hoisted the raven flag and rechristened the sea rover the "Kraken" (a name coined the previous year by Norway's new king, Sverre, for a monster of northern seas often described as half octopus and half crab, and that future generations would identify with the giant squid). He and the lot whom he commanded had developed into a sea king and his pirates, preying upon the commerce in ivory, walrus hides, and other goods between Hvitramannaland and Greenland, Iceland, and like settlements. The number of traders who had not lost a cargo (or something yet more valuable) to Brand-Yngar and his myrmidons decreased week by week.

One day, a large merchant ship traveled on the final leg of a round trip from Vesterbygden, on the southwest coast of Greenland. It was another specimen of the knorr, the most common type of Nordic vessel. Although not of outstanding size (being wider than the Kraken but slightly less than half its length), this particular one was extraordinarily in importance, for its multiple-ton cargo of hides, furs, amber, and other valuables was worth more than the total of the others that Brand-Yngar and his fellow pagans had seized; in addition, there were among the passengers several individuals who might be held for high ransom. As in the case of all their previous prizes, the sea rovers (whose base was on Trinity Bay, on the shore of Avalon Peninsula opposite from Hvitrammanaland, just far enough from the colony to remain secret) had learned of this special ship through stationing a few of the least-recognizable among their own number as spies back among the other Vinlanders.

An elderly passenger aboard the knorr was gazing into a bank of mist that hung upon the water's surface. Just as he was wondering how deeply into the mass his ken penetrated, a large, ominous shape became faintly visible. Like an enormous predator emerging from its lair, the Kraken sped out of the fog; the knorr's male occupants knew immediately that they hadn't the potential to evade the attacker, and so they armed themselves to resist the impending onslaught. As the drakkar drew closer, her crew made no war cries.

At last the ships were near enough one another so that Brand-Yngar could board the trader. He stepped with his right leg onto that one of the fore and aft cargo decks which sat at the bow of the knorr, leaving his left planted within his own vessel (which position, because of the motion of the waves, he knew he could maintain only temporaneously), and addressed his tense audience: "If any one of you wishes to surrender peacefully—or desert to us, as many of your fellows have—him I will not harm; if any one of you should succumb in combat, but remain alive, his life will be spared; but anyone who dares oppose us with insolence and without honor, in his heart shall my sword bury its blade."

Many of the men aboard the trading ship were silent, pondering Brand-Yngar's words, but some began casting derision at his challenge. The subordinate Viking crewmen all had in hand their tools of war, some armed with swords, others with axes, spears, and the like; the shields they carried often bore emblems of heathen Norse significance, such as eight lightning bolts radiating from the center. Brand-Yngar motioned for the attack to begin.

Now filling the chill air with shouts of bloodlust, the pagans swarmed forth from the drakkar onto the deck of their target. Brand-Yngar, in the lead, almost immediately cut down the first opponent to face him. The second to become his foe was a red-bearded man, stout in temperament as well as in build. The redhead, having the initiative, aimed a heavy double-bladed battle-axe at Brand-Yngar's cranium; the rogue captain avoided this blow by hopping sideways onto a rowing bench. With the height advantage that this maneuver gave him, he delivered a slash from his sword that would have left a mortal wound on a weaker adversary. The man with the axe and the red beard slumped toward the bottom of the knorr's hull, his blood staining the wood.

Other Vikings entered the melee; Brand-Yngar knew better than to watch the progress of his fellows while engaged in his own combat, but the periodic glimpses he caught showed that, to his chagrin, the outnumbered and under-equipped targets of the raid were felling many of the raiders. As a result of a missed stroke, the axe handled by one heathen partly imbedded its blade in the knorr's mast; the wielder, having too little time to pull it out, was forced to abandon it to the enemy, who had purposefully let down his guard while his back was to the mast so that precisely this occurrence would transpire. One of the Christians actually succeeded in hurling a hand axe between two warriors and into the body of a third, who was just about to deal a presumably deadly blow to a fallen defender of his vessel.

Brand-Yngar ducked under a weapon-swing meant to decapitate him; instead the blade sliced through a rope fastening the knorr's mainsail to its mast, and the sail fluttered into the air like the tan cape of some sort of gigantic matador. Underneath this canopy, one of the Christians parried a strike from a Viking and retaliated with the unanticipated move of ramming his enemy shoulder-first, bowling the man overboard and into the icy water, where the weight of his own armor sunk him inexorably into the deep.

The man whom Brand-Yngar was currently battling aimed at him again, only to see his sword shatter against the interposed shield. Deftly retreating, he scooped up what was available, a heavy oar, and used it to deflect to the right a swipe from Brand-Yngar's sword. The rearmed man capitalized the shape of the oar to follow up his maneuver, wheeling its other end into the Viking's belly. Brand-Yngar, backtracking to avoid further punishment, thought *Why, he's better off than when he had a sword*. He countered, however, with a blow aimed not at the Christian wielding the makeshift weapon but at the oar itself; the wood split into two pieces. Defenseless once more, the foe simultaneously hurled both halves at Brand-Yngar, giving himself enough time to escape to a different area of the ship.

Brand-Yngar sought to pursue him, but found himself throttled from behind by someone else who had improvised a weapon, the rope that had been severed from the sail. The Christian was positioned so that the Viking leader could not easily stab him from over his shoulder; nor could he hack at the rope itself without wounding himself. Having no alternative, Brand-Yngar repeatedly thrust his sword blindly backward, and also cast away his shield so that he could have one hand free to try to loosen the grip around his neck. Fortunately for Brand-Yngar, superior numbers and more fighting experience were enabling his crew to prevail over the Christians, and several of his men who lacked adversaries converged on the strangler to free their Captain. The holdouts among the would-be saviors of the knorr were subdued.

Now that the strife had ended, Brand-Yngar assessed the situation. The roll of casualties to his side seemed approximately equal in number to that of the losers. Grudgingly, he acknowledged in silence that the adherents of the faith he despised had fought well. While those pagans under his command who were still healthy looted their conquest, he spoke with those who required attention. As he moved among them, one of the knorr passengers caught his ear as well as his eye.

This was a fairly tall young woman, with a generous length of straw-colored hair and eyes as blue as the surrounding sea. She was extremely attractive, especially (in Brand-Yngar's opinion) with her defiant demeanor. Beside her on the deck sat a member of the same sex, bearing a resemblance save that she looked perhaps twice the other's age of 16 years. Her eyes, too, blazed with unspoken indignation as she looked upon her captor.

Seeing that she had Brand-Yngar's overt attention, the younger frostily asked him "What's the matter? Is this the first time you've seen someone civilized?"

Brand-Yngar, taken somewhat aback by the fact that she had spoken first, regrouped and answered "Not one so pretty as you. What is your name, fair one?"

She hesitated in responding, but then told him "Asny Svansdottir."

"She's my daughter," added the elder woman. There was no need to ask the infamous Viking *his* name.

Brand-Yngar dwelt on the name Asny. He liked the pronunciation (AHS-nee), but frowned upon noting its meaning ("new god" in Old West Norse). "You, I suppose, worship the "new god?""

"We worship the only God who has ever existed," replied Asny. "Wouldn't you rather devote yourself to the Eternal than to one who had a birth and will die?" Her final three words referred to the prophesied inevitability, known to all Scandinavians, that Thor and the like would perish in the battle called Ragnarok, the "Doom of the Gods."

"You say the 'only' God," said Brand-Yngar (deliberately ignoring her second sentence, whereto he did not yet have a rebuttal), "but my understanding is that you have three."

"The One exists in three persons."

"How is that possible?" he scoffed.

Asny quoted the Bible: "What is not possible with man is possible with God.' Since He established laws for the sake of the universe, not for Himself, He can supersede them."

Brand-Yngar told her "I wouldn't debate with a gold coin I had taken from a ship's hoard; nor will I do so with you." He turned to the mother and queried as to her name.

"Helga."

"I think I'll call you 'Hel' for short," he quipped, using the name of the heathen goddess of the land of the damned.

Another matter demanded Brand-Yngar's notice, so he left the pair. As he strode away he privately admitted that the brief theological disputation had only bolstered his interest in Asny; a Christian she might be, but he admired character and intelligence in a woman just as much as or more than he did beauty.

The pressing situation to which he was being called was the gathering of ugly weather off the Greenland coast. Hoping to outrun the oncoming storm front back to Vinland, or at least to somewhere they could find shelter from the inclemency, Brand-Yngar directed that the prisoners be rounded up and secured and that the Kraken be made ready to sail due south.

The homeward voyage began in the Davis Strait, to the west of the settlements on Greenland. The southerly Labrador Current certainly had the potential to carry them away, even without the help of oar and sail, but it bowed to the superior force of the rising winds that had already wrecked the knorr. Now gales, they wrenched the Kraken off her course and gave her quite a different heading; the crewmen could not even tell how far they'd been diverted. When they weren't cowering they were praying to Thor for their deliverance, bailing rain- and seawater out of the vessel, or saving each other from being washed over the sides.

Brand-Yngar stood resolute as Captain. Through his decision not to try to reach land immediately he had saved the drakkar from the very worst of the storm; now, he had to guide them through its area of lesser strength to wherever it should capriciously deposit them.

The tempest poured and blustered for hours, driving the dragon ship like a playful godling with a bath toy. Finally it blew the Kraken onto a shore. Yet more time passed before the severity tempered enough locally so that anyone could move about on land; in the meantime the occupants of the humbled watercraft huddled under the cover of their awning, peeping forebodingly at their unintentional port of call.

16

The terrain lacked even a single tree, the ground being covered largely by dark, flat, very heavy rocks. Glaciers were visible on mountains in the distant background. The intense cold of the air, even to Northmen, was almost paralyzing. Brand-Yngar and some others wondered if this might be Helluland, "Stone-Slab Land," which Eric the Red had also accidentally found when sailing from Greenland; it could also be the Vestri Obygdir, which that explorer had described as a worthless land in the west, or a wholly different place. There was no way to confirm or disprove it, but the first speculation was correct, although the location where they had made land was miles removed from that Leif Ericsson's father had first seen. The Kraken was washed up at Exeter Sound, part of the boundary of Baffin Island's Cumberland Peninsula.

At first just grateful to remain alive, the Vikings soon had to confront the problem of finding food in such an inhospitable place; as Brand-Yngar pointed out to his underlings, the provisions they stored probably wouldn't sustain even them alone, much less them along with the survivors from the knorr, on a journey back to Newfoundland from wherever this might be. The most obvious approach to solving this quandary would have been to reestablish their forebears' practice of sacrificing one of every ten prisoners to the marine deity Aegir, but they had forsaken all Norse gods other than Thor; moreover, since their prime purpose in hunting down the knorr had been to take captives to hold for ransom, to simply slaughter the Christians would make their endeavor practically pointless.

It was therefore proposed that a party be sent into the hinterland to replenish the longship. Some of the men addressed their fears to their Captain: "We have more prisoners than ever before, and there are fewer of us than ever before. What if they revolt? They've proven that they can stand up to us. You ought to leave as much of the crew aboard as possible, to fend off an uprising."

One additional reason whereof the men withheld mention was the possibility that those who ventured inland would die there, thus *permanently* relieving the Kraken of several rowers. Brand-Yngar suspected as much, but didn't know whether this attitude might be caused by a genuinely practical concern or by mere cowardice. He was beginning to think that it was not these rogues, but the Scandinavians who had adopted Christianity, who were the true heirs of the boldness the Vikings had displayed when reaching new and mysterious realms. In any event, being more an elected leader than a dictator, he had no choice but to heed the crew's qualms; he decided that he and only two others would conduct the resupplying mission.

Before the expedition commenced Brand-Yngar again encountered Asny, who had no awareness of his pending departure. He did not initially speak, but then, without leading into what he was about to say, asked "How would you react if I were to take you to wife?"

Without facing him, she answered: "I'd rather eat mud."

Unperturbed, he told her "Nevertheless, I just may."

She turned toward him for the first time. "You have the power to do so, so long as you enslave me. But, the one true God won't recognize your heathen ceremony; never will I share your bed until you accept Christ and wed me in a way acceptable to Him."

Brand-Yngar recalled that the wife of his hero, Eric the Red, had given her husband a similar ultimatum. He knew that with his physical strength he could force her to yield to his desires, but, somehow, he didn't feel that he could ever resort to that. He walked away. Asny thought that it was a shame he was an unbeliever, for he was a handsome and in some ways charming man, and one probably not devoid of what Christians would perceive as virtue. She knelt and prayed for him.

The subject of her prayer, and those who would accompany him, clothed themselves as warmly as possible and began the trek inland. They intended to wander parallel to the coast (so as to have an obvious return path), searching for anything that looked safely edible. The wind still blew strongly, but, fortunately, it was at their backs.

Long after they had left the sight of the Kraken, Brand-Yngar and his cohort could see nothing in the bleakness except an occasional skua, ptarmigan, or arctic tern, all of which were too adept at flying to be caught by a party of such limited resources. Nonetheless, since snow did not currently cover the ground, the trio considered that they had a good chance of locating whichever animals had already donned their white winter fur or plumage. They also remembered to examine the nearby shore, knowing that the ocean might provide what they needed.

Later they spotted another avian, but one that seemed to hold out more promise of being caught: a beautiful, black-barred female snowy owl, roosting in a depression in the treeless tundra. On Brand-Yngar's advice, he and the others flattened themselves on the frozen earth and inched toward the bird. As they did so, Brand-Yngar felt hypocritical, for he had recently admonished these same charges of his that "A Viking never crawls!"

The men continued to slide and grind forward on their bellies; if this part of the island had been frosted by snow and ice, they might have resembled oversized penguins. They had approached within a few score of yards, never knowing whether their quarry failed to detect their presence, merely bided its time before taking flight, or perhaps had to stay put to protect owlets, when abruptly its mate winged to the attack from a heretofore unseen post on the summit of a boulder. In silence the golden-eyed, nearly pure-white partner repeatedly and fearlessly swooped upon the hunters, each time wheeling away to strike from a new angle; the flustered Northlanders sought to down the large bird with their weapons, but it maneuvered around the flailing steel, getting its talons so close to their eyes that they thought it very capable of gouging them from the sockets. In frustration, they conceded victory to the owls and swiftly circumvented the area.

As the group trod further along, the air grew noticeably chillier. This did not alarm anybody until one observed that the very storm that had forced the dragon ship ashore was moving northwest. Worse, it now qualified as a blizzard, for the winds were beginning to dust Helluland with snowflakes.

Death was merely a possibility to those staying with the Kraken, whereas it was a certainty here in the midst of a snowstorm; Brand-Yngar therefore instructed the other members of the triad to attempt to retreat to the longship, even though this meant going straight into the powerful and blinding air currents. They saw several animals hiding from the atmospheric fury; to catch these would have been easy, but all their attention was now dedicated to their own immediate survival.

Brand-Yngar felt his legs waxing heavier with each step, and he had no doubt that the rest were growing similarly exhausted; the fact that they had to lift their feet steadily higher to extract them from the swiftly accumulating snow didn't improve matters. During particularly strong gusts it seemed to the comrades that they were barely progressing, for the might of the wind was nearly equal to their remaining determination. Brand-Yngar would have offered words of encouragement, but the frigidity had numbed his lips. He couldn't avoid marveling that he was experiencing a worse blizzard than any he could recall as an Orcadian, where his home had lain at 59 degrees North Latitude, yet this was not yet Autumn! Being ignorant of the Gulf Stream, which brought warm water to his birthplace, and of the Labrador Current, which carried cold water south in the Western Hemisphere, he wondered in his distress if this might be a stage of the Fimbulwinter, the troika of successive severe winters which the sages had foretold would precede Ragnarok.

Hours passed. His associates faltered, first temporarily, and then permanently. Their leader wanted to give them a proper burial, but he knew that to expend the necessary time and energy would merely expedite his own demise. He could only unsheathe each dying man's sword and place it in each man's hand, so that the pair would in Norse belief be granted entrance to Valhalla. Brand-Yngar himself continued onward as long as he was capable of movement, and prayed, as long as he had consciousness, to the deity who as the creator of storms had the power to calm them: Thor. Then, he blacked out.

Brand-Yngar eventually found himself roused, but he did not know the cause. He did not know much of anything till his senses fully returned to him, whereupon he came to understand that a covering of snow had piled almost completely over him, leaving him only a hole through which to breathe. It was this ironic insulation that had sustained him during the indeterminate time since his loss of sensibility. Seeing that the snowstorm had passed, he began to exhume himself from the enclosure.

It seemed, curiously, almost as if something were *helping* to excavate him. Brand-Yngar dismissed it as a delusion inspired by the iciness of his surroundings. He continued to enlarge the opening in what had nearly been his frozen tomb until, abruptly, he became aware of the presence of a very large carnivore.

Just behind him, sniffing to determine whether this find might be palatable, was an animal that he had never before seen: a bear, not so bulky as, but far larger than any in Western Europe, and draped in white fur.

The polar bear, which had hitherto presumed him carrion, clubbed at him with his paw in the way he would crush the skull of a seal. Brand-Yngar snapped his head and torso to one side; the foot-wide paw swiped his flank, tearing away some of his clothing and equipment. Thinking that his only chance would be to draw his sword as quickly as possible and bury it in the monster's forequarters, he slid out this weapon and thrust for the Nanook of the North's neck. Because his stroke was rushed, and thus his aim slightly off target, he succeeded only in wounding the bear. The blade was yet sunk in fur and flesh when the behemoth reacted by rearing up to its two-legged height of well over ten feet, raising the sword along with itself.

Brand-Yngar, now empty of hand, immediately perceived that the predator was standing in order to deliver another blow to the tall human facing it. He had no time to select an alternate weapon, so he moved quickly toward the bear, risking (so he thought) danger of a "hug" but getting inside the trajectory of the forelimb. Its tactic countered, the polar bear bit with its three-inch teeth down toward the Northman; Brand-Yngar blocked the attack with his left arm, which he thought he could better afford to lose than its twin, and used the right to reach and try to pluck his sword out of the animal's sinews.

He didn't get a firm-enough grip on his sword's hilt to extract it as he would have liked, and instead accidentally knocked it into the snowbank. Simultaneously the bear attempted to slam his jaws shut on Brand-Yngar's left arm; because of the height disparity between man and beast, the limb went into its mouth almost vertically rather than horizontally, with the result that even the huge maw could not fit over it. His arm withdrew, ravaged by fangs but still attached to his body.

To stall for time until he could replace his lost sword, Brand-Yngar vaulted out of the mound of snow and ran as fast as he could through the drift, heading on a course that would take him away from the bear in a straight line. The ursine enemy followed, nimbly and with superior speed. The consequence was that Brand-Yngar found himself traveling diagonally toward the ocean; he knew it to be foolish to become trapped with his back to the sea, but the bear pursued him so closely that despite his head start he couldn't afford even a slight change in direction. Brand-Yngar comprehended how rapidly he was losing ground in the chase, only a second or so after its inception, but he could only hope for an opportunity or for a miracle.

The bear was not quite upon the objective of his hunt when the earth seemingly rose underneath Brand-Yngar, jolting him off his feet and sending him sprawling through snow and sliding up ice that lay below it. What he had assumed to be firm, snowbound ground had turned out to be an ice island, blown by the recent wind so that it abutted the shore, and the polar bear's mass was tilting it down at this juncture. The section where Brand-Yngar lay was correspondingly tilting up, and so gravity drew him back across the slippery surface toward the waiting jaws of the polar bear. During his descent he took into hand his backup weapon, a throwing spear, which he had not been able to use before in the fight, and rammed it straight down the gullet that was expecting to taste flesh instead; the 16-inch head pierced the wall of the bear's hungering throat and brought its life to a close.

The small section of sea ice, no longer tipped by the sudden impact of some three quarters of a ton of polar bear weight, returned to its previous flat position. Brand-Yngar removed his spear and recovered his sword. After a while of staring in wonder and profound respect at the dead predator, he knelt and (deeming it wise, regardless of his exhaustion, to start before scavengers discovered the corpse) began to skin it with his only other weapon, a smallish knife. The situation of the carcass, which he could not hope to move by himself, obliged him to carry out most of this work on the ice floe.

At last, despite the difficulties, it was complete: he had fashioned from bear hide some rude garments, including a tunic and cloak, to protect the wearer from such a severe climate as this one. In the meantime he had intentionally exposed his wounds to the same climate, so that the glacial air would stanch the bleeding; what loss of blood he did incur, though, teamed with his great exertion of late to make him nearly as weary as he had felt just before he lost consciousness during the blizzard. Another factor was psychological: knowing how long a walk back to the Kraken was impending. He tried to force himself to stay awake, but he just needed rest so desperately; the curtain of sleep descended unnoticed.

When Brand-Yngar finally rose from his requisite slumber, he saw through the cracks between his eyelids that the surroundings had changed. Starting up, he perceived that nearly everything around him was either ice blue or aqua blue. The Arctic wind, as so often before, had reshuffled the flow edge; he was drifting once again. The polar-bear carrion was not present, having slipped into the ocean after the platform of ice was carried away from Helluland. Brand-Yngar felt angry with himself, not so much because he was lost in a freezing sea as because of the loss of this possible source of food, whereto he could have directed the Kraken. At least he could determine from the motion of the sun that his transportation was heading eastward, generally toward the ship; perhaps, he thought, this would turn out to be an unexpected bonus by allowing him to conserve energy during his return trip.

After an unknowable length of time he discerned that his crystal raft was approaching land. The land in question seemed no more hospitable than any other he had seen in the past weeks, but it supported some life forms whose shapes he could barely see from so far away. He waited eagerly to take a closer look, but soon observed that his floe was no longer sailing in that direction. Fearing that he might never have another chance to reach terra firma, he gambled that he could jump from here to the closest plane of ice, which was somewhat nearer the coastline; from there he would try to leap to another, then to another, and so on. To fall short or simply lose his footing would mean immersion in the water, the temperature of which was scarcely higher than that of its frozen version.

He delayed and changed his orientation until he was positive that his back was to the wind, so that it would help rather than hinder his attempt. A running start made it a success; he strode to the farthest edge of his new icy abode and endeavored to repeat his maneuver. This time he slipped during the dash that preceded his intended saltation. Fortunately, his momentum didn't take him over the brink; he started anew and on this occasion cleared the gap (although his feat did end in a crash-landing).

Brand-Yngar was about to continue hopping toward his destination when, having come close enough to the terrain to see its inhabitants faintly, he discovered that they were another unfamiliar species of creature. Size was very hard for him to judge from this distance, but the beasts were much larger than human beings, weighing as much as 900 pounds and measuring up to five feet tall at the shoulder. They were swathed in thick wool; their large heads sported horns which curved down and then back up before tapering to a point, and were so broad at the base as to form a sort of helmet. They resembled cattle, but were not exactly bovine, having some characteristics also of sheep and goats. He was seeing for the first time a herd of musk oxen.

As soon as his squint showed him that these animals had horns, he began to feel that he might have been better off staying far from land. He was downright alarmed when he heard a crash, and then understood the cause of the resounding noise: the musk oxen were rutting bulls, head-butting each other's thick and hard skulls to establish supremacy.

Brand-Yngar saw only futility in trying to retrace his leaps back to the starting point, so he watched impotently, hoping that the current wouldn't carry him straight to the strand where this jousting was taking place. The drift continued steadily, though, and ultimately he came so close to the animal warriors that he could smell the musk whence comes their name.

As late as the moment when his natural raft ran aground, he couldn't tell whether the musk oxen had seen him. The question was then immediately answered, for he had not yet placed either of his feet on the tundra when one of the hotheaded males turned to face him, snorted, and charged. When the rush began the musk ox was some 20 yards distant, but it closed the gap surprisingly rapidly for such a heavy animal. He hurriedly drew his sword, but even before he did so he could feel himself anticipating the onslaught with eagerness rather than with a healthy amount of fear. Although he didn't know why, he now scorned danger and uneven odds, and felt glad and proud that he wore no armor nor used a shield. As the horn-mad animal lowered its head in closing to the attack, Brand-Yngar, intoxicated with adrenaline and desiring to see blood spill forth, lunged to meet it, thrusting his blade between its eyes and through its skull. The momentum of the charge forced him to backpedal and fall on his ice conveyance, and furthermore loosened the sword from his grip, but he recovered quickly enough to notice the next threat: another bull, equally large and foul of temper, galloped toward him.

Brand-Yngar extricated his weapon from the slain individual, but did not have time to return to the permafrost before this new challenger attempted to gore. The ox stepped onto a partly melted and thus thinner area of the ice, accidentally penetrating it with its hoof and halting its own advance; he availed himself of the stroke of luck by springing to the beast's flank and burying cold iron in its leather hide. As the quadriped succumbed, the breach that its heavy leg had made in the floe widened. The weight of the other dead one contributed to what was obviously becoming the disintegration of the weakened glaze. Two others, their fury heightened by the action they had witnessed, hurled toward him almost simultaneously. Brand-Yngar hurdled over the prone oxen's bodies and away from the opening cracks. As soon as he landed he switched the sword to his left hand, clasping the right about his spear, which he then launched toward the nearer of the two chargers. The cruelly pointed head struck home. He fitted his now-free hand over the other on his sword's hilt, and so delivered a two-armed blow that cleared the surviving ruminant's head armor and sliced through the nape of its neck. Again the musk ox's power knocked him onto his backside, and it also shattered the glinting blade. He paid this event no heed, but regained possession of his spear and ran at a herd member that had not even behaved aggressively toward him. The titan turned and attempted to flee, but Brand-Yngar cast his spear; the missile lamed it in one of its rear legs, whereupon he caught up to it and finished it off by stabbing its throat with his dagger. The musk oxen he had not killed sped away, not wishing a closer encounter with this frenzied man.

Brand-Yngar, his lust for violence subsiding, stood awhile in stupefaction over his own feat and how he had accomplished it despite his previously sustained wounds and other factors. He had heard yarns concerning the berserkers, men who went into battle wearing not armor but merely bear sarks (shirts of bearskin) and relying on pure ferocity for victory, being imbued (or imagining such) with the spirit of the brutes that had previously worn the skins, but he had never met one; now, it seemed, he had become one. This was the first experience he had ever had that he could describe as supernatural. He gazed down at his white raiment and marveled.

Brand-Yngar returned to the Kraken by following the littoral route south. When he terminated his absence by announcing that meat (a savory variety, although no one could have predicted that) awaited them farther up the coast, nearly all aboard hailed him as a savior; the mourning for the two who had accompanied him was genuine but proved no match for the jubilation felt even by Christians over their deliverance. Although in an expansive mood, he found occasion between the accolades to sneer at Asny "I prayed not to your god but to mine, and he saved me. I'm more convinced than ever before that yours is a false religion." During the long-delayed voyage back to familiar territory he married her in a traditional Nordic ceremony, involving swearing by the name of the goddess of love vows.

Several months went by, during which Brand-Yngar kept raiding and Asny kept a vigil of prayer for his conversion; it was now 1002. One day he was relaxing alone in the Newfoundland woods, as was his wont. He still wore his polar-bear pelt, which he had adopted as a trademark since the phenomenon relating to the musk oxen, although it had not worked similar magic at any time afterward.

As he laid spread out on the grass, watching a pair of ravens or crows engage in acrobatics high above, they ended their aerial maneuvers and flew closer to him. Brand-Yngar expected them to alight in a tree or two, but instead they came still closer, so much so as to capture his interest as well as his attention. He felt fascination yet uneasiness as the birds actually perched on the ground close by him. He could now see that they were in fact ravens, and quite large even for their species. They trotted until they were almost near enough to touch him, whereupon he rose to a standing position and found himself protesting "Have you come to peck out my eyes? See, I'm not dead."

To his disbelief, one of them responded: "We know you aren't, Brand-Yngar Magnusson."

"What sort of beings are you?" His sword hand was ready on the hilt, but then he recalled that the chief god Othin reputedly had two talking ravens, Hugin and Munin, whom the deity sent out to spy and to communicate his messages to mortals.

The other fowl spoke: "The Father of All has dispatched us to tell you that he has chosen you, a mere man, to assist in his great work. You shall help to prepare for the final battle."

Brand-Yngar, still half spellbound by this otherworldly occurrence, took in the words as deeply as he was able. One of the designations for Othin was

"All-Father," and the last battle ever to take place would be that of Ragnarok. He asked the feathered speaker "How am I to do this?"

"By slaying the Serpent who Encoils the World."

Brand-Yngar was flabbergasted when the import of the words reached his mind. The nicknames "Coiler," "Coiled One," and "World Serpent" applied to Iormungand, which had resulted from a union between a giantess and the evil god Loki, the "Father of Lies" and enemy of the good members of the Norse pantheon. Since the monster was divine progeny, Othin and those aligned with him could not legally kill it; the head god therefore had instead thrown it into the sea, where it had grown unchecked till it circled Midgarth (the entire human realm). According to prophecy it was still in the ocean depths, and would remain there until Ragnarok, when Thor (despite the prohibition) and the colossus would destroy each other.

Brand-Yngar was speechless, so the winged messenger who had first spoken added: "It is because you are not of the godhead that he has selected you. If you defeat Iormungand your god shall not have to die, but live."

Having sunk to his knees, but finally found his tongue, Brand-Yngar queried weakly "Where do I begin?"

"To fulfill this quest you will need better weaponry. You can obtain a sword, shield, and helmet at the knothole where dwell the dwarves Blaengir, Brynrik, and Uxi in Svartalfheim. Armor you have already, for you are wearing it."

Brand-Yngar pondered these extraordinary statements. Svartalfheim, "swarthy-elf home," was, like Midgarth (which lay directly above it), one of the Nine Worlds of Norse cosmology; the swarthy "elves" (also known as black elves, Dvergar, and dwarves) who inhabited it were stumpy, grudging, greedy, ill-tempered, magical, sun-shunning troll-like persons who lived underground or in hollows of very large trees. There were two races, one of which was the Durin, fashioners of mighty magical arms of war; they were known to forge these for the relatively well-behaved deities such as Thor, but never did so without demanding something highly valuable in exchange. It was undoubtedly these with whom he would be dealing. He was more confused in regard to the "armor" of mention, but one of the ravens, reading his thoughts or anticipating his question, croaked: "That, you will soon comprehend."

He continued to mull over what he had heard, and then offered: "I pray the lord Othin not to be angry with me for asking just one more question: how do I reach this knothole?"

"The answer is simply that you must fare forth." With those words the avian team spread their wings and departed from him.

Brand-Yngar had great difficulty thinking about anything other than one subject for long after the ravens had left. He stayed in the forest until the men he commanded began to wonder and worry about his whereabouts. In his opinion it was good that no one (at least no non-celestial person) knew how to find him when he went on these private forays, for he ultimately concluded that he might as well begin the practice of Seith (faring forth, or soul craft), to which the ravens no doubt referred. This meant that his soul would leave his body and thereby be capable of traveling to other of the Nine Worlds in the company of a spiritual guide. It would unquestionably prove perilous, but his chief reason for reluctance was that Norsemen regarded it as feminine; no less a figure than Othin had been accused of degrading his manhood for indulging in it, and Brand-Yngar would certainly have balked at the idea outwardly (as he did inwardly) had the instruction not come from a god.

He returned to the Vikings' camp to let his presence reassure everyone that he still lived, and at dusk secretly set out to go to a place near that where the ravens had located him. In the meantime he had clandestinely acquired what he hoped would be a sufficient amount of knowledge and material for his spiritual journey. With one exception these materials comprised a scroll inscribed with magic formulae, and a small skin pouch and its contents: teins, both to serve as herbs and to provide a magic wand, and a few trinkets and other odd items that would likewise serve as charms. The sole exception was that he would of necessity sit on a High Platform; he obviously could not bring this along, but he knew of a natural mound in the wood that would serve well enough in this capacity. Because this "trance travel" would be strictly personal, however, he could not involve one recommended element of the ritual, which was having a circle of women sit round the Seith practitioner.

When he reached a point roughly halfway between home and his destination, he saw in the dying sunlight something he had not known to exist in that area: a waterfall of perhaps 10 feet in height. A chain bound a young, attractive woman to a stone at the bank of a pond formed at the foot of the falls. She beckoned him closer; intrigued, he did as she had bid him. As he came near enough to see her face he almost mistook her for Asny, for this stranger bore a strong resemblance to his wife.

The maiden whispered in fright "Please help me, sir; a man who lives here is keeping me prisoner and seeks to force his will upon me. Be my champion, and free me from him."

Brand-Yngar was just about to whisper back in order to inquire about the "here" where she had said the man lived, for there seemed nothing about the place that even remotely appeared like a human habitation. He was cut off, however, by the instantaneous emergence apparently *through the waterfall* of a smallish individual wearing a coat of mail and with a hand ax hanging at his side. The stranger folded his arms contemptuously and said "Well? Will you be her champion?"

By unsheathing his sword Brand-Yngar answered the challenge without speaking a word. When his foe made no effort to advance toward him, however, he snapped: "Is this how you plan to prolong your life, knave? Come up onto dry land, so I can kill you in proper fashion."

The mailed warrior disdained to move or even to issue a retort. The woman tried to impart some information to Brand-Yngar, but in the excitement of pending battle he interrupted her to give the instruction "Make taut your chain"; she could not but obey him under the circumstances, and with a Herculean, overhand blow from his sword he clove the iron bind nearly in two. Upon seeing this, his antagonist splashed forward with as much agility as almost anyone else would show on land; the Asny look-alike cried to her defender that the man was "a fossergrim" (an enchanted being who could not miss an opponent when standing in water), but the warning came too late to avoid the joining of combat. Brand-Yngar, caught unprepared by the speed of the advent of the fossergrim (who still waded ankle-deep in the pond), could not evade the swinging ax; it struck him obliquely but strongly in the chest.

Both belligerents assumed that this sole stroke would finish Brand-Yngar as well as the fight. He felt blunt pain from the force of the stroke, but no penetration, for his polar-bear hide had somehow turned back the edge as if composed of metal rather than leather. He now knew the meaning of the raven's statement that he already possessed armor.

The damsel knelt down and struggled to separate the partly severed links that still held her fast. Brand-Yngar returned a blow for the one he had just sustained, and his had more effect; the ax-wielder staggered away from the bank. Then, though, he regained strength and again aimed his ax at his land-borne adversary. Having learned a lesson from his previous attempt, this time he struck a body part unprotected by the white fur, drawing blood. Brand-Yngar essayed to drive through the man's mail with point of sword but failed, and the fossergrim once more put his ax to work. Brand-Yngar intended to use his sword to fend off the slashing blade, but this tactic inexplicably had no effect; the fossergrim's weapon struck home, but fortunately did little damage.

"You can't beat him when he's in the water!" shouted the woman, just as she succeeded in freeing herself from the chain. "You must take him from his waterfall!" Brand-Yngar could not immediately heed the advice, for he was at that moment attempting to deflect another strike from the hand ax, and with no more success than he had had with the first parry. He was beginning to see that while his hide armor might negate the effect of a blade hewing at his trunk or upper arms, he could do nothing to prevent the weapon from making contact with him (and he felt himself weakening). At his next opportunity to try to smite the aquatic foe he instead hurled his sword directly at the man's face; the fossergrim easily knocked the substitute missile out of the way, but in doing so gave Brand-Yngar time to lunge from the shore and enwrap him with his arms, pulling them both beneath the pool's surface.

The bodies of the grappling pair reemerged, with Brand-Yngar still in control. As easily as he could when handicapped by mud, water resistance, and the fight remaining in his adversary, he lifted the fossergrim above the water and carried him to the turf. "Remove him as far as possible from the falls," the woman called to her hero; "I'll show you the way!"

He followed her, and the cascade diminished in their view until it vanished. The trek took the three through a forest path that Brand-Yngar did not know; he wondered how much farther he would have to drag the fossergrim, whose efforts to break the Viking's grip were causing him great strain. She led him onward for some distance further until there appeared a clearing ending in a cliff. Panting, Brand-Yngar forced the man to the edge, and with a final burst of energy tossed him to the foot of the high precipice. The fossergrim lay stretched out and did not rise.

Brand-Yngar stared down over the brink till convinced that he had eliminated the threat, then turned to address her whom he had rescued; he was speaking to someone who was no longer within sight. Recording the episode mentally as just another queer experience to have befallen him of late, he reversed his route from the fossergrim's lair, reacquired his immersed sword (rust, though not yet visible, was on its way), and confiscated the enemy's hand ax as well. He needed healing for his lacerations, and since the torch on his person was now too damp to light his way through the waxing darkness, he was compelled to return to the Vikings' haunt.

After a night and day rife with restless anticipation, the subsequent evening he repeated his eventful traverse, this time making it beyond the waterfall. Under the twilit sky Brand-Yngar reached the raised earth that he had selected as his "high platform" and smudged much of it with mugwort he had brought to provide purifying smoke. He seated himself at the center, in order to fulfill the ritual step called "sitting out," and began a series of chants purposed to sanctify the area and to cause one to enter a meditative state. He would have to iterate the rather extensive monologue nine times or until the desired effect came to pass.

He had long since lost count of how many rounds of the chant he had completed when he heard a recognizable voice softly call his name. Fearing to disrupt his semi-consciousness, he cautiously opened his eyes just wide enough to see who had spoken. The face matched the voice; it was Asny, or her perfect likeness, for even the maid he had met yesterday did not so closely resemble his wife. This reminder of the previous day's encounter troubled him, for the fossergrim had enslaved that unknown woman just as he had unilaterally espoused Asny.

In a way the sight now before him was indeed Asny, for it was a fetch, an apparition of a living person; in Seith doctrine this was not a separate entity but a manifestation of a part of the forth-farer's own soul (this brought to Brand-Yngar's mind a Bible verse that his wife had often quoted in regard to married couples: "And the two shall become one"), usually of the opposite sex, who would serve as a guide through the spirit world. The Asny-fetch invited him "Let us begin your journey, Brand-Yngar Magnusson, for you have far to go."

Having been surprised to see his beloved in such circumstances, he already was on his feet and ready to travel. "Take my hand," she offered, and when Brand-Yngar did so he found himself suddenly in an altogether different sort of locale. In fact, it was as if he were not part of any world but, rather, removed from all the Nine Worlds, and able to see most of them at once. The mythological concept his elders had taught him held that each World occupied its own place among the trees or branches of the astronomic World Tree Yggdrasil, but that at the same time each could be viewed within the context of geography. Indeed, Asgarth (the heaven of the gods and of the bravest heroes to have fallen in battle) could be seen in Asia and Jotunheim (a land of various Jotuns or Ettins and most other giants, both good and evil) in the vicinity of the Arctic ice pack.

Details of this fantastic cosmos became visible to him, and so he could now see entities who had been in Midgarth all along but who had remained outside his perception: guardians, in animal and various other forms, of natural places. Asny ventured no explanation, but Brand-Yngar took them for landvaettir, who served precisely this function in the pre-Christian beliefs. He had not yet realized that he had also attracted the attention of one of the personal, baneful spirits known to the Norse heathen as meinvaettir, as well as the countering protection of a benevolent one designated in myth as a dis. The duo had in fact already begun influencing his life; the latter, in addition to checking the malevolence of the former, was invisibly warding away the assaults of such monsters as draugr (the undead, capable of causing death to the living), trolls (noxious, inhuman terrestrial beings), and Huldru-folk ("hidden folk," people of the wilderness who often captured mortals through the use of cunning and magic).

Brand-Yngar had officially achieved the status of seithmath, a man who went on spirit journeys; he was now too awestruck and fascinated by his circumstances to feel any shame at what opinion other Vikings might have. Without using human means of locomotion, he and Asny somehow traversed the immeasurable space that separated them from Svartalfheim; it was as if they had progressed through the focusing lens of a telescope. Once their feet had restored contact with the ground, he saw that he and she stood encompassed by such an expanse of the new world that none of the other eight could still be seen. The surroundings did not abound in greenery but rather in shades of gray and brown, for the black elves had no use for the Sun's rays or for the flora that thrived on its energy.

Asny guided him through the drab scenery until a leafless tree loomed in the distance. So high did it tower that after they first caught sight of it, ten minutes went by before they reached its base. Brand-Yngar could see the knothole that, Asny assured him, was the one he needed to enter in order to find Blaengir and the other dvergar. It was above ground level, but here the tree trunk sloped from the sky at an angle gentle enough so that he climbed to the orifice with only a little danger of losing his balance. As he was about to disappear into the tree's interior he savored a last look at Asny, since (though attached to him, in a non-physical way) there was no need for her to accompany him through the aperture, and noted that this semblance of his wife provided just as much comfort to him as she would have were she with him in the flesh. He gave her a faint smile and crouched to enter the elfin lair.

Slouching all the way through the dwarf-sized tunnel in the wood, he came to a dim chamber (the smoke-darkened roof whereof his head almost brushed) that housed a diminutive forge and the hollow's trio of wizened, hunchbacked occupants. All three had been laboring on some kind of metal artifact when Brand-Yngar's intrusion drew their notice. "Who are you?

How did you get here? What do you want?" demanded the ugliest of them, Blaengir, in a croaking voice.

"Brand-Yngar Magnusson; faring forth; weaponry I need for a mission of Othin," came the reply to all three interrogations.

"Ah, yes," snorted the misshapen speaker. "The gods of Asgarth have yet another task for us. I doubt very much that you'll succeed in slaying Iormungand no matter what sort of equipment we give you."

"I'll wager he'll be lucky to pierce even one of its scales," added Brynrik.

"Probably won't even get near enough to take aim," sneered the third.

"In fact," cackled Brynrik, "He—"

"*That's enough*," snapped Blaengir, scowling at both. He returned his attention to their visitor and then moved into another room, leaving Brand-Yngar alone with the rest and wondering how to converse with dwarves, the remaining two of whom the first's rebuke had made even more sullen than usual. A few minutes later Blaengir came back, now in possession of a helmet. "This is all we'll give you right now," he said, handing it to the human, "because it's all we *have* to give so far. We'll have something else ready if and when you return from Hel's domain—with Fjalar."

Brand-Yngar had been told to expect that the black elves would charge a steep price for their service, but he was nevertheless aghast. Fjalar, heroic by dwarven standards, was a selfish and unsympathetic member of the Durin race who defended his people from giants and other enemies. Brand-Yngar hadn't heard that Fjalar had died, so Blaengir gave him a whitewashed explanation of how this death had occurred, portraying the event (which had actually resulted from over-imbibing) in epic terminology. As the three dvergar curtly sent him on his way, he left the knothole in profound silence, imagining (while trying not to do so) how it would be to rescue someone from the chthonic fief of the horrifying goddess Hel; he vowed to never again call Asny's mother by that name.

While he clambered down the sloping trunk he stole occasional glances at what the black elves had given him; so thunderstruck he had been by the exorbitance of their demand that he had neglected even to inquire about the helm's properties. It was a handsome piece of armor, bristling with two horns from an aurochs (Brand-Yngar had no way of knowing that someday people would think typic Viking headgear looked this way), but impressed him as being too large to stay atop his shoulders.

Now back on the ground, he decided he ought to try it on before going too far from the dwarves' dwelling. When he placed it over his head, with Asny looking on, it shrunk to fit him ideally. "The black elves have great magic indeed!" he exclaimed. He verged on saying more, but was cut short by the coming into his mind, evidently from a source outside his body, of a message that communicated the other strengths of the helmet. The helm itself was telling him that it conferred superhuman vision and hearing upon its wearer and that it could withstand shocks strong enough to rive one of more mundane manufacture. Pleased almost enough to forget about his upcoming visit (that is, he *hoped* it would be only a visit) to the place called Helheim, Niflhel (not to be confused with the hyperborean Niflhe*im*), Helgarth, or, after its ruler, simply Hel, he removed it until the time should arise when he expected to need it.

As Asny explained, the next major instance of faring forth would differ somewhat from that previous, since neither Brand-Yngar nor anyone else but the soul of a dead person could attain the Nordic Hades in such direct fashion; he would first have to go to the point of Midgarth's convergence with the rainbow. To believers in the Nordic gods this phenomenon was Bifrost, the bridge from Asgarth to Earth and on to the Underworld. Even that path, however, would not bring him all the way to Niflhel.

The pair spirit-voyaged back to Midgarth, but then had to make a prolonged journey into the west before arriving at the terminus of the rainbow. Brand-Yngar passed the whole trip in silence, for how could he speak when he was about to embark on an adventure the equal of any related in the Sagas? Here he was, barely over 20 years of age, setting out to brave the nether world, from where many supposed not even a divinity (trance traveling or otherwise) could return. Notwithstanding his obligation to Othin and love of adventure, he found himself wishing that their trek would last indefinitely, that he and his mate could spend the remainder of their lives just strolling through nature in seclusion from the rest of mankind. (Partly because of his sense of bewilderment since receiving his godly commission, it had already escaped his mind that, according to Seith doctrine, his corporeal form had never left that Newfoundland mound that he had made his "high platform.") The end, of course, did ultimately come; before he knew it, and without really knowing how, he was now taking his first, trepid step into one of the dales that he would have to cross as the first part of his foray into the unknown.

This valley consisted of such depth, and so close to total blackness approached the dark which soon enveloped him, that he could no longer see his fetch or even himself. Only her voice comforted him with her presence. The next rift through which his course lay was as lugubrious as the first; the third was the same, as were the fourth, fifth, and so on. For nine days he lacked even the least significant illumination, but so long as he had Asny to keep him on the correct path he stood no chance of becoming lost in this bizarre realm.

At the end of the ninth day the two came to the Gjoll River, which flowed out of the iced-up spring Hvergelmir in Niflheim (the inconceivably cold, farthest north of the subterranean regions, where dwelt frost giants) and completely encircled Helheim. No one could cross this fluid barrier except at the point closest to them, where it was spanned by the Gjoll or Hel Bridge, thatched with glinting gold but quite flimsy. Because the light in this area was merely dim, Brand-Yngar could see the guardian of the unsound structure: the enormous, ghastly, man-devouring ogress Modgud. Fearful but resolute, and constantly murmuring prayers to his god, he went forward.

As the flooring creaked under his weight without giving way, the inhuman sentinel turned her gaze toward him and the woman at his side. She had been sitting, but now rose to confront the wayfarer with her muscular arms folded. As soon as she stood he could see that her height equaled that of the polar bear he had flayed seemingly an eternity ago; as he drew closer more details of her appearance became clear to him, such as her muddy-brown hair and the fact that she bore warts on a disproportionately large nose and protruding chin. She measured about the same in girth what she did in height.

He halted. "What is your name," Modgud boomed at him, her face bearing an impassive expression, "and of what family are you?"

She had posed these questions to everyone else who had come her way, because, like other peoples of the antique world, the Northmen considered ancestry to have great importance regarding one's identity. He answered: "Men call me Brand-Yngar, the son of Magnus who was the son of Gunnar, the son of Rathulf the son of Bjorn, the son of Unn the son of Ottar, …" He concluded the oral parade, which comprised multiple names of chieftains, with "…the son of Sigurd of Jotunheiml, the son of Thor."

The gorgon replied to his genealogy with: "Descended from those others you may be, but not from Thor; nor does your line have its origin in Jotunheim." She then moved so that she was parallel with and on the left side of the Bridge, making it evident that the sojourner was free to continue through.

Brand-Yngar didn't know quite how to respond to her surprise statement. Why did she dispute whether his earliest known forefather was a man named Thor? He also contemplated explaining that he had spoken not the word "Jotunheim" but "Jotunheiml," alluding to a locale in Norway. He thought it

34

unwise to correct an ogress, though, especially one who didn't show any particular hostility toward him, and so he bypassed her without any commotion. From the Gjoll River's opposite shore the road stretched yet lower and northward to Hel's nine dominions, where, he reasoned, he would have more-than-ample challenges to face.

Brand-Yngar and Asny followed the pathway until they finally could see their mile-deep goal, and what a sight it was. Before them loomed the forbidding, massive, stone Hel Gate, known also as Death Gate and Helgrind; Hrimnir, a rimthurse or frost giant who sat by this fortification to serve as a watchman; Hvergelmir, a terrible mountain where the dragon Nidhogg devoured the damned; Ari, a giant who had taken the shape of an eagle, overlooking this tenebrous, chilly, foggy world, frightening the incoming dead, and sharing Nidhogg's dining habits; the four-eyed, most baneful wolf-dog Garm, guarding the island of Lyngvi whereon Loki and the elephantine Fenris Wolf were chained in the cave Gnipahelir; the hall Nastrond on Dead Man's Shore, a place whose north-facing doors no sun reached, covered by serpent skins and dripping venom through its chimney, where traitors, adulterers, and murderers waded woefully in a frigorific stream and provided food for Garm and Nidhogg; and tumuli, graves, by a gate to the east.

The blood-smeared Garm espied Brand-Yngar and Asny at a distance, and issued a howl that sounded to them as voluminous as had the storm they had undergone in the Arctic Ocean. This not only added an emotional chill to the physical one Brand-Yngar already felt in his extremities, but also alerted bestial Hrimnir to his advent. He affixed his dvergar-constructed helmet and continued forward. Hrimnir clasped his gargantuan club, reminiscent of an oak tree or the mast of the Kraken.

When he finally came close enough to see Hrimnir fully, he concluded that this frost giant was even more frightful than Modgud. He was more hideous yet, and far larger, easily two times Brand-Yngar's stature. Like the others of his race he was malformed and close to witless, but that didn't mean he was incapable of doing battle.

Brand-Yngar also kept an eye on Garm, whose howl had subsided but who was now baring his fangs, slobbering, and snarling in his direction. He was bound on Lyngvi Island, within the lake Armsvartnir, but (since he guarded the entrance to Helheim as well as that to Gnipahelir) probably not bound *to* the islet; the length of the chain, and the fact that Hrimnir would not even bother to interrogate him as had Modgud, inspired Brand-Yngar as to how he might neutralize both giant and giant wolf-dog.

Brand-Yngar thought his best hope of defeating Hrimnir would be to initiate the strife. As Asny stood several feet away, he feigned a servile bow and then plucked his sword from its scabbard, using a continuation of the motion to thrust his blade toward the frost giant's belly, which was the only vulnerable spot he expected he could reach.

Hrimnir did his best to straighten and attenuate his hulk of a body, with the result that the sword merely punctured his leather belt; then he kicked the sole of one of his feet against Brand-Yngar's chest, knocking the attacker a few yards in reverse. He had managed to hold on to his sword, but had fallen supine. Garm, excited by the burgeoning bloodshed, leapt over the channel of water separating him from the scene of the action, pulling his iron tether almost taut and moving shudderingly close. Now that there was enough space between the belligerents so that he could wield his cudgel, Hrimnir lofted the prodigious weapon and brought it down with enough force to crush a god, let alone a man.

Brand-Yngar somersaulted forward inside the trajectory of the blow, which thumped loudly but without detriment on the dirt where he had lain. From his knees he struck out a second time, not at Hrimnir's midriff but at the giant's right leg. The sword's edge carved flesh; Hrimnir cried out in pain, but had too solid a build to buckle from the assault. He raised his club to again attempt to punish his diminutive foe, but Brand-Yngar was so near that this proved ineffective. Brand-Yngar struck again, causing a deep wound in the same limb, which he had rightly guessed was the one wherein Hrimnir had more dexterity. The frost giant attempted to kick as he had before, not with his harmed right leg but with the unscathed left, and because of inferior coordination he only glanced his target. Brand-Yngar shifted toward his own left before repeating his attack, for the dual purposes of negating the danger from the massive gamb and of completing part of a circle intended to turn the giant around. Hrimnir spun to keep pace with him, cast away his practically useless club, and swiped with his freed right hand at the human's head. Although it hardly made contact, the brushing would have broken the neck of someone clad in a helmet of poorer quality; as it was Brand-Yngar only lost his balance for a split second, and then turned further in order to continue his strategy. Garm was so close that Brand-Yngar could smell his fetid breath and feel drops of his saliva.

Once more Hrimnir felt steel sever his blood vessels. By now he could barely stand on the ravaged one of his legs. He made a greater effort to reach down quickly, and this time closed a scabby and filthy hand around his tormentor's waist. Brand-Yngar drove his sword into the mammoth wrist of the arm controlling him, effecting his prompt release; while Hrimnir tried to stanch the copious hemorrhaging from his upper limb, the human used the gap between the column-like calves as a shortcut to the giant's rear. The combatants were both facing Garm. Brand-Yngar summoned all his muscle strength and, from his new position, executed a mighty two-handed slice with his deteriorating blade, which created a furrow through the flesh of both of his opponent's lower thighs before his momentum waned. Hrimnir toppled forward; because of his substantial height his head and shoulders fell within range of the ever-greedy jaws of the watchdog, which entertained a taste for frost giant as well as for man. While Brand-Yngar and Asny hurried away from the gruesomeness, Garm set to devouring his fellow warder.

Helgrind was unlocked, since it was the means whereby the dead gained entrance to their permanent home; presumably, thought Brand-Yngar, the presence of Garm, and formerly of Hrimnir, was enough to keep out those who did not belong there. Although titanic, the gate balanced so adeptly that his strength sufficed to push it open wide enough for him to slip through. Asny came along, and Brand-Yngar shut the great door as tightly as he could to seal off all reminders of the grisly scene he had left behind.

Upon turning away from the gate he beheld a new sight, for the Hall belonging to Hel (or Leikin) herself had not really been visible from the exterior of Helheim. The homestead Eliudnir, known more descriptively as Damp With Sleet, boasted very high gates and tremendous walls. It occurred to Brand-Yngar that the goddess he would probably encounter was sister to Iormungand, the very "worm of Midgarth" that Othin had enjoined him to destroy. He speculated as to whether this deity of the dead knew of his assignment, and in a low voice sarcastically reflected "A superb way to ingratiate myself."

Turning back would have availed him nothing except perhaps avoidance of death, so he went toward the fortified construction. While he did so, he realized to his consternation that he had suffered minor but real injuries in fighting Hrimnir, although he ostensibly had traveled not in the flesh but in the spirit. He didn't understand this, but was in no mood to query his company about the matter.

To surmount the last barrier to their foreboding destination the couple had only to open Drop-to-Destruction, the stone door leading into Hel's stronghold, and cross the doorstep Fallfordarv. Brand-Yngar put his hand toward the portal, but with maddening slowness it began opening from the inside; standing opposite him, when the process came to its protracted end, was Damp With Sleet's resident manservant Ganglati. He too was a giant, but his length of stride didn't help him to rush about; his name translated as "tardy," and as when observing a reptile it was often difficult to determine if he were alive. *On the other hand*, thought Brand-Yngar, *is anyone in this Hall truly alive?*

He stepped through the opening and tried to affect a swagger partly for Asny's benefit, but mostly for his own, as they left Ganglati far behind. A macabre splendor marked the decor here, for the chambers he entered and exited were, as he had heard in the legends, rivers of red gold; jewels hung on the walls, and even the curtains dubbed Gleaming Bale indeed gleamed at the same time they bespoke balefulness. The furnishing made sense, for this was not the place of torture for the evil but of eternal gloom and boredom for those who deserved neither paradise nor an inferno.

All at once his self-tour ended and he found himself at the rim of the cavernous Banquet Room, where Hel shared her provisions with the myriad souls consigned to her dim abode. At the far end, amidst innumerable others currently feeding, but easily visible because of her unique appearance, lurked Hel herself.

She had already fixed her gaze upon the visitors, if one could call it a gaze, for her worst feature was not her state of being gigantesque but that of being partly dead and partly alive; half her body was as black as midnight and the other consisted of pallid flesh, the face on that side being wholly blank. Her overall proportions, though huge, pleased the eye, and someone with very bad vision might even have called her attractive. She sat as mistress at the head of a very long table, eating off her dish called Hunger and with the knife Famine.

Brand-Yngar looked around, but there seemed no hope of locating Fjalar in such a crowd. Knowing that Hel had spotted him but wondering if she might not discern between him and the legitimate members of the dead legion, he decided to just stroll around until he found the dwarven warrior or something else transpired. While he thus wandered, evaluating the option of sampling the drab fare in order to better fit in with his supposed fellow cadavers, Hel rose from her chair. Immediately she attracted the attention of all who supped with her.

"I know you are a stranger," she announced without designating Brand-Yngar as the subject of her words. The departed souls gradually realized who it was whereat she stared, and in the meantime he endeavored to select a course of action.

"If you know that," he at length called back to her, "perhaps you also know why I have come." Since he stood so scant a chance of finding Fjalar on his own, perhaps she would unwittingly find the black elf for him. In case she should in fact have no knowledge of his mission, he added "I must retrieve Fjalar, the champion of the Durin, to fulfill a quest given me by the king of the gods."

"No one, once here, can ever leave my household. That includes you, Brand-Yngar."

He had hoped that she'd consider his reason ample for making an exception. As a divinity in her own right, however, she apparently did not consider All-Father's authority absolute. Now, it seemed, he would have to persuade her to make *two* exceptions.

Many of the dead finished their dinners and began emptying the hall. An armored, whiskered figure, slightly over four feet in height, left his seat and said: "I am Fjalar." He strode toward Hel and at the same time deftly slipped on a pair of metal gauntlets, never looking away from the death goddess. "She refuses to release us, my friend, but release we must have. How shall we free ourselves?" He paced yet closer, and answered his own question: "I propose that we do so the same way anyone has ever achieved anything else; by force!" With his last two words he hurtled forward to strike Leikin, and pummeled his target with his characteristic iron gloves.

Brand-Yngar hadn't time enough to think how lucky he was to have an ally who didn't need to smuggle his weapons, since they were also articles of clothing. He instead rushed to join in the attack; as he slid his sword out of its scabbard, some oxidizing parts of the edge crumbled away. Fjalar abruptly described a half circle, so that he could bludgeon Hel from behind and hopefully force his human partner to take up a position in the unprotected front. Some of the shades who had remained in the area tried to help in order to, as it were, take over the kingdom of death; they lacked an effective means of fighting, however, some having armor but none having arms, and when they attempted to overwhelm their mistress (who *was* armed, with a sword) by the weight of their number she simply batted the crowd away with her left arm and returned her attention to Fjalar's potential rescuer. Most of them fled (*For what*, thought Brand-Yngar; *their "lives?"*) to other chambers of Damp With Sleet.

Fjalar again hammered Hel with his mailed fists, one immediately in succession to the other. Although he stood much shorter than a man, his broad build and magical gauntlets enabled him to hit with even more force than did Brand-Yngar, who was wishing he could employ the same strategy he had pursued versus Hrimnir; his comrade-in-arms, though, was in the way.

Hel, the mother of maladies, had the potential to thus infect anyone with a simple wave of her hand, but she could not do so and combat her diminutive opponents at once. Therefore she swung her blood-grooved sword straight down at Brand-Yngar, who dodged it. He lunged closer in an attempt to reach her with his own weapon. She, unlike Garm's newest meal, was tall enough, and her blade comparatively short, so that she was not similarly handicapped when fending off a foe in close range; she parried his thrust, making much of his body vulnerable to assault. She followed up on her advantage not by counterattacking, however, but by looking over her shoulder to locate Fjalar and then stomping at him with one of her huge feet.

Fjalar escaped being crushed thanks to his miniscule size. Hel snapped her head back to the front to see what her human adversary was doing, and brought her sword down to slice him in two. Brand-Yngar, on his back, rolled to one side; the edge struck the ground. He observed that the blade shuddered upon hitting the stone flooring, although so much strength did her wielding arm have that rock fragments flew from the floor itself.

Brand-Yngar vaulted onto his feet, but made no attempt to approach Leikin any more closely. She tried once more to fight off the dwarf who was inflicting damage, albeit non-lethal, on her from behind. Brand-Yngar waited for her to launch her next attack at his own person, knowing that the height difference between them meant she could not skewer him but would rather have to repeat her attempts to slash downward. He purposefully left himself exposed; as soon as the sword had reached a point in its arc where he wagered Hel could no longer alter its course, he moved away. Iron dug into stone, but this time stone emerged the victor, for the blade, weakened by the previous such collisions, shattered into several pieces.

Hel, flustered by the development, sought to continue the combat unarmed. Fjalar, whose bravery no one could fault, went on punching with his specially gauntleted knuckles; Brand-Yngar, at his earliest opportunity, latched his arm around the black elf's and hauled him away. "We don't need to kill her," he shouted at his warlike companion while running for the exit from the scene of the struggle; "our victory will be getting out!" In fact, Brand-Yngar could only guess at what might result from the death of the goddess who ruled over death; perhaps dying would become a thing of the past, disrupting the order of the universe.

By adroitly weaving around and between those of her subjects who remained in the area, and coursing in a crouching position so as to be almost unseen among them, the pair and Asny fled the dining room faster than Hel could follow. Relying on the fetch's unerring guidance, they sped through the various chambers Brand-Yngar had explored on his way in, ultimately passing through Drop-to-Destruction. While crossing the terrain between there and Helgrind Brand-Yngar remembered that (although now safe from Hel, who would not be able to leave her abode until it came time for Ragnarok) they would need to get by Garm yet a second time, unless the wolf-dog were sleeping off its sizable meal. The legends held that one who had fed the poor of Midgarth could placate the canid with one of Hel's cakes, but Brand-Yngar had had neither the thought nor the chance to secure one while escaping from Eliudnir.

As they discovered when pulling open and clearing Hel Gate, slavering Garm had full sentience; it bounded over from Lyngvi Island as if it hadn't fed in days. Brand-Yngar had expected him whom he had rescued to aid him in fighting off the beast on their way back to the land of the living, but Fjalar seemed unprepared to meet the challenge. Garm sprang toward the dwarf's throat, which had the protection of armor, but the monster bit with such force that his grimy teeth pierced Fjalar's defenses and sank into flesh.

Brand-Yngar couldn't accept so cruel a turn of fate. Had he really just sallied successfully into the stronghold of death only to see his mission fail this way, mere seconds later? If Fjalar were to die here, still in the Underworld, his mortality would not be revocable by any known force. The black elf fell to the ground with Garm's formidable jaws still clamped around him; Brand-Yngar tried to react but knew that he could not do so in time to prevent the occurrence of what he had feared. He felt boiling within himself the same rage that he had when faced by the musk oxen on Baffin Island. He threw aside his shield and began dealing the carnivore one prodigious sword-blow after another. Garm reeled from the onslaught, leaving behind its prey as well as much of its own blood; so rapid was Brand-Yngar's hewing, one stroke following the next almost as if it were part of the same motion, that the canine barely had time to retaliate. When the fiend did bite at him Brand-Yngar started battering its head, at once further wounding it and neutralizing its means of attack.

Garm generally moved backward, but occasionally would lunge. By the time its antagonist had spent his furious vigor it had managed to make contact several times between its jaws and his body, but on each occasion Brand-Yngar's bearskin held out against serious injury to its wearer. At last Garm acknowledged defeat, turned tail, and leapt over the watery boundary that fringed Lyngvi Island. Brand-Yngar, panting and incapable of following the guardian over icy Armsvartnir, had no qualms whatsoever (once he came back to his normal state of mind) about seeing it go.

He felt no contentment, however, over what had befallen Fjalar. It was thus to his surprise when Asny enlightened him: "You assume too much, Brand-Yngar; he yet lives. Garm's mouth is so large and Fjalar's neck so small that it didn't succeed in tearing out his throat. If we return him to the dvergar in time, he may survive."

Brand-Yngar therefore could not spare the time to recuperate, but with Asny's assistance began transporting Fjalar away from Helheim and the spectral denizens thereof. Modgud did not hinder them as they recrossed the Gjoll Bridge. The couple did their best to stanch Fjalar's profuse bleeding by plugging it with part of his clothing and exposing his wound to the cold; it occurred to Brand-Yngar to use the chill waters of the nether world for this purpose, but he discarded the idea when he recalled the reputation of at least some of these rivers for toxicity. He hoped also that on the return trip they might encounter a giant with the capability of magically healing the black elf (but, even so, how would they persuade him to work this magic? Any such being would likely be as avaricious as Fjalar himself, and extort an unpayable price).

Ultimately Brand-Yngar and Asny returned to the three dwarves' knothole, with Fjalar barely existent. Uxi first noticed them struggling to scale the tree trunk without jolting or dropping the dwarf hero, and excitedly alerted Blaengir and Brynrik to the fact. Uxi and Brynrik peered out of their opening into the twilight, taking up most of the space at the mouth of the entrance tunnel and evincing shock at Fjalar's condition, but Blaengir forcibly parted his way between them and gazed down at the three figures. Without offering assistance, he sneered "Is this how you treat our champion? He looks half dead!"

"Then he must be improving," replied Brand-Yngar, trying to secure a foothold on the thick bark, "because he's usually looked closer to 95 percent. Do you think you could take time away from your spectating to help us?"

Brynrik and Uxi cringed at the prospect of venturing outside their wooden cave while there still was some luminescence outside, but Blaengir shoved each from behind, sending both tumbling down the decline. Blaengir zipped back into the shelter; with the hands of the other two dvergar added to his, Brand-Yngar finally managed to hoist Fjalar to the level of the knothole. Asny again stayed behind, but whispered advice to Brand-Yngar before he made his own ascent and then groped his way inside.

Brynrik and Uxi carted Fjalar into the cavity that served as a smithy; Brand-

Yngar followed closely. "His wound must be festering," he warned them, "and he's barely breathing." Directing his statement chiefly at idling Blaengir, he remarked "You have power to cure him; how strongly must I urge you?"

Blaengir hasted into another room but then seemed to stay there longer than he had during Brand-Yngar's first visit. Uxi and Brynrik creased their brows to a still-greater degree than was ordinary, so deep was their worry over Fjalar; Blaengir protruded his head from the pitchy darkness and called to them "Bring him in here."

The subordinate black elves did as he had bidden them. After a long while, Blaengir stormed into the forge room where Brand-Yngar awaited the outcome. Uxi and Brynrik were with Blaengir, but looked sad rather than angry.

"Fjalar has died," he snapped. "You have failed in your quest. You'll get nothing more from us; in fact, I must insist that you hand over that helmet I've already given you."

Brand-Yngar felt great consternation at what had transpired, and bowed his head in sorrow. When Blaengir tried to snatch away the lowered helm, however, he refused to allow the dwarf to lay his hands on it. "You charged me with getting Fjalar out of Helheim, and that I did; he was outside Helgrind when Garm inflicted the mortal wound. Besides, if you had acted decisively you might yet have saved him."

Blaengir was incensed. A rod lay with one white-hot end in the forge; he palmed the opposite extremity and thrust the searing metal toward the face of Brand-Yngar, who ducked under it. The improvised weapon clanged off his elfin helmet, whereupon Brand-Yngar adeptly unsheathed his sword and plunged it into the chest of Blaengir, who quickly died.

The other dwarves, stunned and terrified by the happening, dropped to their stubby knees and pleaded for their lives before Brand-Yngar. Gravely he said to them "I will certainly spare you, so long as you treat with me more faithfully than did this Blaengir. I expect you to give me what he vowed you and he would at the close of my mission."

Brynrik and Uxi nodded their heads solemnly. "The truth," said the latter, "is that nothing is yet even available to give you, for Blaengir had intended treachery all along; he never expected you to return to Svartalfheim, and so he didn't make anything." Brand-Yngar was not surprised at this, since it was the possibility of dishonesty against which Asny had cautioned him before he revisited the black elves' womblike dwelling.

Brynrik added: "I feel that your claim is just," and Uxi assented. "Therefore we will forge what you need, a sword, a dagger, and a shield." Uxi cracked a faint smile and said, largely to himself and to Brynrik: "Really, there's no reason why we can't craft them just as well as if Blaengir were still in charge. It will, though, take a few days."

Brand-Yngar granted them the time they said they needed, keeping ready to pursue vengeance just in case the pair should renege on their word (they were, after all, of the same basic nature as Blaengir). When it had elapsed they demonstrated their trustworthiness in this instance, for they presented him with three beautiful items. The sword measured nearly 40 inches from pommel to point; its hilt (the crossguard of which was of modest breadth, and the pommel similar to a cap) was sculpted from rich bronze and decorated with such Scandian cultural motifs as stylized birds, a composite of runes together denoting "higher self," a sort of dragon that archaeologists would dub the "Jellinge beast," and a picture of a seaborne funeral showing Vikings ascending heads-downward to Valhalla; the blade was partially incised with a "blood groove," the purpose whereof had nothing to do with blood but merely with decreasing the weapon's weight, and carved into it were runes that spelled the military arm's name Ufaellin (Dauntless). His new shield, replacing that he had left behind outside Helheim, bore a central spike so that it could play a role in offense as well as defense; from there radiated the three segments of the Nordic symbol called a triskele or triskelion. The whole shield qualified as a buckler, for it was circular and of median size. Finally, the dagger was similar to, although, of course, more brief than Ufaellin, but had detailed etches seemingly everywhere, along with a red gem of uncertain identity (Brand-Yngar surmised that the dvergar knew more about it than he, but forgot to thus inquire) in the middle of the creature-headed hand guard. Despite not having had a chance yet to test the weaponry's effectiveness, he could not but be pleased. Even if they should prove hindrances in combat, they bespoke high value merely as treasures.

Brand-Yngar had no desire to start a fight for the sole reason of proofing his new equipment, and so he instead tried first the sword (after contemptuously flinging away its rusty predecessor) by using it lightly against a tree there in Svartalfheim. The ease wherewith it cut through bark and xylem amazed him. Clearly its edges were harder and sharper than if it were of human manufacture; he speculated (accurately) that its makers might have forged from adamant, the philosophically theorized unbreakable substance. Next he examined the shield, noticing with only passing interest that it did not, as did so many others, bear the protective runic inscription of the war god Tyr. He acted out a shield rush toward a pretended enemy, using as a substitute the same tree he had maimed wielding Ufaellin; the lethal projection penetrated with surprisingly little effort. He had yet to assay only the dagger. Based on the experiences with the other two weapons he thought he knew what to expect from this one, but nevertheless targeted that same poor tree, and found that when he drove in the blade the wood yielded readily. He gave the dwarves the full amount of thanks he thought they deserved for such spectacular gifts, and then he and Asny embarked from the plane of Svartalfheim for that of Midgarth.

Brand-Yngar was back at the place whence his adventure of faring forth had begun, when he thought on the fact that he now had everything the ravens had said he would need to battle the "Worm of Middle Earth." He knew he ought to feel confident, in view of the fact that he had received his calling from the god who was above all others, and that he had contended successfully (even without most of the supernatural aids he now possessed) with monsters and the forces of darkness; he did not, though. He cursed his lack of faith, and sought to uncover the truth about his future through a standard means of divination called rune casting. Asny waited as he dallied.

The runic alphabet supposedly provided people with revelations through the cryptic significations of its letters, but it gave Brand-Yngar only confusing and contradictory answers. He mentally searched for a germane augur instead through the sagas and lays which had nurtured him, and recollected that a "man of power" could in legend travel to Asgarth by merely touching the rainbow Bifrost and wishing to go there, obviating any need to fare forth. Did he not qualify as a "man of power" from having engaged the enemies of Othin? Did he dare take the initiative of using this transport to appear before the Norns, the counterparts of the Greek Fates, to question them about the destiny they had established for him? He delayed his action further while he mulled this option, Asny remaining patient. Abruptly he realized that, in a peculiar way, he feared the potential consequences of not knowing his fate more than he did those he thought might result from making such a move without obtaining permission. He reminded himself that, as elders had taught him, his religion forgave its adherents easily; any wrongdoing of his could be effectively erased through success in a future battle, providing of course that he should live to fight said battle. He chose not to ponder the matter so thoroughly as to risk coming up with an answer he didn't want; he *would* return to Bifrost and proceed thence to Asgarth, unless someone greater than he should specifically enjoin him not to do so.

Brand-Yngar knew that he would lose his fetch upon returning in spirit to his true, corporeal body; therefore he considered it fortunate that Asny had already shown him the way to the end of the rainbow, so that he wouldn't actually need to rely on her guidance while journeying there. This turned out to be moot, however, for when he announced his plan to her she remained loyal without divulging what opinion she might have of the matter; anyway, he valued her mere company and expected to need her direction once within the realm of the gods, and so did not attempt to end his trance traveling.

He and she went to Bifrost in the same way they had before, but now he was even more restless than he had been the previous time, and the rainbow bridge yet more breathtaking and inspiring. From the outset he beheld part of this object that was his destination; as he and Asny progressed it increasingly revealed itself beyond the hills and over the treetops, and (when his eyes were not, as often, on her) he excitedly tracked the minutest degree of what from his perspective was its growth.

Finally Bifrost nearly filled the sky, because Brand-Yngar and Asny stood at its Earthly base. The sight was spectacular, since a permanent sheet of flame surmounted its seven colors, barring giants, ogres, and other undesirables from using it as a venue for invading Asgarth. The bridge itself was thinner than one might have expected, so much so that it could not bear the weight of Thor, who therefore had to reach the world of the Aesir (the chief race of gods; the other, called Vanir, comprised those who dwelled in a different world called Vanaheim) by a less convenient route. Brand-Yngar, weighing some 190 pounds, didn't doubt that it would support his sub-divine self; he could not help feeling uneasy about the carpet of fire, but he tried hard to trust in the legends. He held Asny's hand with one of his own and put the other to the rainbow.

Instantly some unseen force levitated him, his fingers still in contact with the bridge. He passed through the interposing pyre unharmed and found himself and Asny on that length of it beyond the burning wall. Brand-Yngar gazed toward the far end of the rainbow, but it was too remote for him to view and blocked by clouds besides. He started to walk up the arch, maintaining his balance without difficulty. All awareness of time gradually became lost to him during his fantastic ascent through an enveloping atmospheric ocean, replete with aerial currents.

Brand-Yngar and Asny drew closer to the clouds until at last they apprehended Bifrost's summit, at the entrance called Othin's gate, a drawbridge which permitted access through an almost unbreachable wall of tightly fit stones (it was said to be constructed from the "limbs of Leirbrimir," a clay giant) and across the rapid Asgarth river. Few could solve the lock of the portal, and should anyone bring the door out of its place in the wall, where it keeps out those individuals not allowed to enter, the very gate would in some extraordinary way become a chain for him. On Brand-Yngar's and Asny's side of the circumscribing stream, immediately opposite the drawbridge that these objects defended, projected ramparts wherefrom it could be lowered to span the foaming fluid. Complementing the fortifications, a dark metallic-colored, shimmering, inflammable sort of haze called vaferflame floated above the eddies of the citadel's de-facto moat; the same material as the source of lightning, it had an inhuman sapience which ensured that it aimed its fire at him for whose destruction the gods kindled it and that it never erred in hitting its mark.

A solitary person stood before the cordon. The large, strong figure wore armor even whiter than the pelt that clad Brand-Yngar, and had teeth of gold. He carried a fearsome sword and a horn, called Gjall, that he would someday use to signal the onset of Ragnarok by sounding it so loudly that every living thing in all the Nine Worlds would hear it. Brand-Yngar identified him as Heimdall, the "White God" of light who kept an unceasing vigil over the rainbow bridge.

Since Heimdall reputedly had hearing so acute that he could even hear grass growing, and vision infinitely superior to that of any eagle, he indubitably had detected Brand-Yngar long before the latter (even with his special helmet) had observed the former; yet it was now that the "Son of the Waves," as others also named this watchman, blew Gjall softly to announce the coming of a visitor. "If you were a giant changed into the semblance of a man," he explained to Brand-Yngar, "you would not have this lady by your side. You may pass." He went to lower Othin's gate.

Brand-Yngar thanked him and offered him a gracious bow; when he straightened up he could see in the background, through the now-open gateway, Heimdall's horse Golden Forelock and his splendid hall Himinbjorg. Asny showed him the way beyond these and into the Golden (or White) Kingdom, as some knew this place, a dominion perched in the high branches of the Tree of Life (an alternate designation for Yggdrasil). Generally similar to Midgarth, sharing its omnipresent reminders of the divine, it nevertheless far exceeded the Earth in beauty.

Another series of peregrinations, through fields interspersed with groves and woods, culminated with Brand-Yngar's and Asny's sighting the gargantuan trunk of the cosmic ash tree. Shadowed by it, there stood the fabulous Hall of Fate, dwelling place of the Norns; in its vicinity sat these "Weird Sisters," which appellation referred not (although it could in justice be thus applied) to their strangeness but to the fact that they formulated for every other being his weird (derived from the earlier "wyrd"), the original sense whereof denoted "destiny."

As Brand-Yngar and Asny could see when they drew close enough, the Norns sat by the swan-inhabited Urda Well, drawing water therefrom in order to tend Yggdrasil and spinning the threads of mortal lives. Here the divinities of Asgarth would hold court. The Urda (or Weird's) Well, proximate to one of the cardinal roots of the World Tree, similarly took its name from the source of "wyrd," as did Urd, the eldest of the Norns. With her silver distaff she wove the past of other creatures; the other two, younger Verdandi and still-younger Skuld, labored at producing threads which respectively bespoke the present and the future. The trio of humanoid but inhuman females stood for the three stages in a woman's life: pre-pubescent, childbearing, and beyond menopause.

The Weird Sisters naturally knew of the visitors' approach, but paid them no notice until Brand-Yngar entreated from a few yards away: "Great Norns, you know my wyrd. If you will divulge this to me, I will give whatever recompense I have the ability to give."

Verdandi glanced but then went on weaving, and Skuld acted to raise more water from the Well, but Urd faced him and uttered "This we will do, Brand-Yngar Magnusson, in return for a favor."

Brand-Yngar shuddered inwardly at the prospect of another quest, but braced himself for what the seeresses would demand. Urd continued: "Many dragons gnaw the roots of Yggdrasil, which we are trying to keep alive; we request that you eliminate merely one of them, Grabak, in exchange for your prophecy. He is the one nearest to here, and so to find him you need only follow this root downward."

Brand-Yngar could not follow the root *directly* downward, but thought he might use that information to locate Grabak once he had reached the place by an alternate route. Having familiarity with the story of Wayland the Smith, he knew that this legendary figure had dwelt, in the Wolf Dales, near one of the passageways leading down to Niflheim. He expected to experience various hazards in the course of reaching this entrance to the Underworld, for the Wolf Dales existed at the northernmost limit of the Earth, in the wastes bordering Jotunheim; outlaws such as Wayland might choose to live in such barrenness, but the gods never went there even momentarily.

By the time Brand-Yngar and Asny arrived in the Wolf Dales they had indeed had to undergo trials and suffer adversities of the various sorts whereof one must keep wary when wayfaring to such a desolate reach of Utgard, that is, all the worlds lying beyond that of the Aesir. The two came upon the traces of Wayland's habitation, a house by the lake Ulfsjar (Wolf sea) and an indication that they would not have to fare much farther to their goal of the tunnel entrance. Because of the unfriendliness of the terrain itself, they encountered no unfriendly inhabitants thereof before the mouth of the nether region yawned within their ken.

Unlike the knothole in Svartalfheim, this opening had a diameter sufficient for Brand-Yngar to ingress without stooping; indeed, at least one giant had followed this very route to Niflheim, but this knowledge brought some discomfort, since it meant that something or somebody of that size might be returning from there now. Brand-Yngar nevertheless undertook the descent, in the company of Asny.

The couple initially passed by or brushed the roots of the few plants hardy enough to grow in the humus of this severe borderland; as they slowly moved deeper nothing but minerals met their inspection, except for occasional bones of men or of monsters. Having heard the account of the said giant's precedent, Brand-Yngar fully expected the trip to be as lengthy and laborious as it turned out to be.

Throughout, Brand-Yngar and Asny didn't espy a single living thing; even the earthworms, he mused, had enough sense to avoid such a dreadful place. It was with both relief that he and she had reached the end, and foreboding over what precisely might lie beyond this terminus, that Brand-Yngar finally exited the conduit and stepped into Niflheim.

Like its sister world Helheim, this one was dim and gloomy. Niflhel was merely chilly, though, whereas the freezing of Niflheim surpassed that Brand-Yngar had undergone even in Helluland or the Wolf Dales; he hadn't known that cold could reach such an extreme. He certainly felt gratitude for the otherworldly warming power of his bear-fur garments, although he would have wrapped Asny in them if she were not, as a fetch, indifferent to climates.

Hoar frost coated every surface of the cavern that now filled his sight; had there been more light in this dismal place, the rime would have scintillated. Immense Grabak was not in view, but Brand-Yngar detected the ominous noise of chewing emanating from some distance. Moving cautiously because of the lack of light and the unsure footing, bewaring especially of the danger that he might slip and impale himself on the many inverted icicles that acted as crystalline stalagmites, he shuffled in the direction of the mastication sound.

Eventually he turned a corner into another ice cave and beheld the expected root of the Tree of Life. The whale-sized reptilian he had come to find sprawled before it, his back to Brand-Yngar and Asny, munching nonchalantly. The fiend was of an unpleasant, close to nauseating mossy shade of greenish brown mixed with gray; on its head it bore horns, and its skin comprised rough-looking scutes, some as large as a human fist; a fork was the shape of its tongue and an arrow that of its long tail, and from the tips of the toes on each of its six feet protruded a talon like a marlin spike; its eyes glowed an infernal red. *I can handle this easily*, Brand-Yngar unpersuasively told himself in thought.

His next thought concerned the probable futility of the action he was about to undertake. *After all*, he spoke mentally, *here I am, soon to combat a serpent, and for what purpose? To hear whether fate will grant me triumph over yet a different serpent?* At the same time he recognized that he had come too far to abort his effort. Building his inner resolution to carry on, he hurtled forth to strike Grabak while its countenance was still turned from him.

Ufaellin cut through the armor of the dragon's midriff thanks to its superior point and edge, but since its length limited its penetration, it did not sink deeply enough to fulfill Brand-Yngar's hope of damaging an internal organ. Grabak spat out a mouthful of xylem from the Tree of Life, roared its displeasure, and lashed with its tail at the offender positioned at its rearmost pair of legs.

The limb did no more to Brand-Yngar's fur-clad body itself than leave bruises, but its momentum swept him toward Grabak's most deadly part, its jaws. The monstrous worm (by which term it and other dragons, like Iormungand, were often known) expected to be able to leisurely scoop up the would-be slayer and thus supplement its vegetable diet. Brand-Yngar, however, recovered from the battering swiftly enough to use his shield to neutralize the ensuing bite. For good measure he took a hack with Ufaellin at the beast's forelegs; as it had an ample number of such appendages left, he had no illusion that this would seriously damage his antagonist, but at least it might serve to distract him. As Grabak withdrew its head some of his saliva spilled onto the hoary ground, creating a fuming pool.

While Grabak reacted to the foiling of its maneuver, Brand-Yngar darted in a semicircle until he was at a side of Yggdrasil's root opposite that where the dragon had fed. He had opted to move there merely in order to use the enormous plant as a barrier between himself and the intelligent reptile, so that it would not be able to use its fiery breath against him for fear of scorching its food supply; he now noticed, though, that what wood remained unconsumed bore the same stubs one would find on any root of ordinary size, and that because of recent feeding the plant's devourer did not have a slippery coat of frost. The nubs were large and rough enough so that a man could use them for handholds when climbing, which he promptly did upon sheathing his sword.

As Brand-Yngar scrambled without sacrificing too much safety for speed, he thanked the gods for the inspiration to divert Grabak's attention by slashing one of its legs; perhaps he had thereby gained the time he needed to ascend high enough to attack a vulnerable area of its head. The worm craned its long neck in an attempt to search him out. It extended and bent around the root, but saw nothing because it was looking at ground level. Brand-Yngar continued to clamber upward, repeatedly stabbing into the flesh of the root with his dagger and spiked shield in order to lessen his dependence on the knobs and thus boost his rate of progress; he already had reached a point so high that if he were to fall he would risk serious injury.

Grabak had its head below him, but swivelled it so rapidly that Brand-Yngar dared not try to let go and land on it. Then, the serpent spotted him; its huge jaws opened wide enough to engulf him whole.

As it grew closer the gape came to resemble the ice cavern that Grabak inhabited, for although colored garnet instead of white and silver the length of its dentition equaled that of short stalactites. Excepting his shield, which was strapped to his left arm, Brand-Yngar had only one weapon in hand: his dagger, which would not deliver him from being snatched off the root by the worm's teeth. He felt he had just one option.

Brand-Yngar sprang off the World Tree, not away from but right into the menacing maw. This enabled him to bypass the fangs (as well as the venomous drool) and come to a sort of rest on the forked but soft tongue, which he then furiously assaulted with his knife. Rather than swallow him as it had intended, Grabak spat him out, sending him sailing diagonally to the cave floor.

The angle of his descent and the lack of friction on the icy surface lessened the impact on him, and caused him to skid many yards from where Grabak had ejected him. He was now back almost at the place where the combat had originated, parallel with the firedrake's vent. Grabak again visually roamed the environs for its enemy, and found him, but before it did so Brand-Yngar hurtled to his feet, employing his own lurching movement to draw Ufaellin, which he would need as a substitution for his dropped dagger. He bounded and ultimately dove to the frosty floor, his momentum carrying him to a spot underneath Grabak's rib cage. Brand-Yngar thrust the engraved blade into the carnal roof above him, lacerating the worm's innards.

Grabak roared, the echoic walls of the ice dungeon multiplying the noise's volume. The serpent's foul blood spurted forth, and the whole creature showed signs that it verged on collapsing. Brand-Yngar had to run and crawl out from under the mammoth body just as quickly as he had gotten beneath it, lest he be crushed; he narrowly escaped.

Brand-Yngar knelt, because of his exertion and of his desire to credit the divine powers for his victory. He did have to cut the orisons short when he realized that Grabak was persisting in its death throes, and that he and perhaps even Asny might thus be endangered by its miasmic exhalation; he sent her out of the subterranean grotto and then evacuated himself, after staying only long enough to retrieve his dagger.

The gurgling of wintry water rising in Hvergelmir spring became faintly audible now that Grabak no longer gnawed on Yggdrasil's root. Brand-Yngar as well as Asny knew that similar abominations were present there, and so he stifled his curiosity about the object, and paced back to the channel at the obverse end of which were the Wolf Dales.

Forth-farer and fetch returned safely to the abode of the Norns, who, as the overseers of destiny, already knew that he had performed the service they had required of him. Brand-Yngar, therefore, had no need to pose for a second time the question concerning his wyrd. "Your fate," Urd told him, "is not to destroy the World Serpent but to contribute toward his downfall. In doing so your own death will come to pass."

Urd calmly returned to drawing water from her namesake Well. Brand-Yngar left with Asny, not replying in word or even in thought, for what could one say in such circumstances? No one could ever accuse the Norns of partiality.

He hearkened to the fact that the goddess Idunna, who dwelt not all that distant from here in the dells of Idavoll (the Field of Ida), in the midst of Asgarth, gave away one of her Golden Apples to each of the Aesir every year; without these magical fruits, contained in an apparently unremarkable wicker basket, their undying-status would end. Once already, by making his initial trip to Asgarth, he had acted in a way that might have fatally postponed Othin's commission to him. Should he again put himself in jeopardy of divine wrath by trying to pilfer one of the Apples?

Brand-Yngar came to realize that the ardent emotions he had felt over hearing of his imminent death had prevented him from thinking clearly, for Idunna's Apples conferred *youth* rather than *immortality* (immunity to perishing not merely from old age but also from any other cause); moreover, he now reacquired his cognizance that not even his gods could alter the Sisters' decrees. Yes, he concluded, he would simply have to further dedicate himself to his role as a warrior and focus on the Viking tenet that by dying with weapons in hand he would, if sufficiently heroic, earn a place in Valhalla. In this heavenly hall, Othin would personally host feasts for the most valiant of the slain; indeed, the arch-deity would adopt these "einheriar" as his sons. In between their banquets, at which they would receive an endless supply of precisely the same sort of victuals that they had enjoyed in Midgarth (specifically the flesh of an extraordinary boar of Othin's, perpetually cooked, eaten, and restored to life), they would train to war for the gods in the Battle of Ragnarok by sparring versus each other on an adjacent field, all their wounds being healed when the fighting ended. A heathen Northman could hope for no better afterlife, and Brand-Yngar had previously aspired to it, but by now he longed for more; he didn't know whether he ought to ascribe this sentiment to the surety of his forthcoming demise or to Asny's describing the destination of Christian souls as a paradise rather than as a mere place of food and fights.

While he had yet to leave the Golden Kingdom the ravens Hugin and Munin reappeared to him, to instruct him to embark as soon as possible on Skidbladnir. This ship, a lending from the god Yng (the source of the first element of "Yngar'" although Christian, his parents had given him this name to customarily honor a member of the extended family), would not even need a helmsman or crew to bear him unfailingly to a certain pelagic area, in the deep whereof squirmed the Midgarth Serpent.

Brand-Yngar grimly began his obedience to the dictate by exiting Asgarth and making his way toward the bay, in a part of Midgarth that he did not recognize, where the ravens said he would find his designated transportation. Although back in the world that Brand-Yngar called his own, he still needed Asny to pilot him to the proper place.

The avian ambassadors had not lied; he arrived at the titanic, unmanned, passenger-lacking argosy, and immediately after he and she boarded the vessel it transported them (sans wind for its sails) with godly swiftness to somewhere over one of the shallower depths of the local continental shelf. In Brand-Yngar's opinion this actually happened too quickly, for he could not savor his final seagoing moments at the pace he had anticipated. He dwelt on the expectation of nevermore smelling the salty surf, hearing the gulls cry as they wheeled above, or even seeing the rage of a storm. Not only did he not find any interest in this newest of the long line of wonders that had been shown him, but also fate had denied him a last chance for appreciation of the Earth's everyday marvels.

Skidbladnir slowed and halted. The voyage had to this point been as smooth as any seafarer could expect, but Iormungand perceived something lying on the surface and so shifted his stupendous coils, causing a seaquake. The waves that this catastrophe created rocked the ship terribly, to a degree that it would undoubtedly have capsized any such construction not owned by a divinity. Brand-Yngar experienced great hardship trying to hold on to the things whereto he successively clung, first the rigging, then the mast, and lastly the tackle and cords, and then the hydrodynamic power washed him entirely off the deck. A whitecap sucked him into its trough and all of a sudden he submerged, spinning head over heels.

Fortunately, another property of his dwarf-crafted helm (aside from being waterproof, like all the rest of his equipment, and the fact that no force could wrest it from his head except when he willed this) was to enable the one who wears it to breathe underwater (or in choking smoke, or under similarly trying conditions). Thanks to the superb vision that he already knew it gifted him, his gaze penetrated the current envelope of bubbles, foam, and aquatic life speeding away from the violence.

Once he distinguished up from down he swam deeper. He did not yet see Iormungand, and the light decreased in brightness with the increase in deepness, but again the effect of his unusual helmet provided adequate visibility. He had little knowledge of water pressure, but his bear armor resisted it anyway. Still he descended, to a level from where, when he checked behind himself, he could see no indication of the surface. His progress continued, and then his eyes met the most awesome sight yet.

Iormungand, so vast that even Grabak looked an *earth*worm in comparison with it, prostrated on the ocean bed; it grasped its tail in its mouth and thus formed a loop engirding the Earth. The proportions of the World Serpent not only came close to defying exaggeration but also benumbed Brand-Yngar, for none of the anecdotes, yarns, and fables he had heard about this spawn of Evil had prepared him for actually seeing it. The only illustration of its immensity he could perhaps make would concern its head and the features thereof, the only one of its body parts entirely encompassed by his scope of vision; in his estimation this member alone would not have fit inside the Niflheim lair where Grabak had harried the root of Yggdrasil.

Brand-Yngar plotted to blind the monstrosity by hewing away at its eyes, so that he might subsequently attack by surprise. Iormungand, however, released its tail from its bite, unhurriedly bent until its snout pointed at him like an envenomed arrow awaiting discharge from bow, exhaled a column of bubbles, and lowered its jaw. Thousands of gallons of seawater rushed to fill the created cavity, and in only a few seconds' duration this great influx sucked him into the recess of the horrid mouth.

The Coiler snapped its jaws shut and promptly refastened them onto its tail. In the total, liquid-filled darkness the power of Brand-Yngar's helmet did not avail him; he tried to orient himself by groping for the dragon's tongue, but no sooner had he done so than the archfiend initiated the swelling of its mouthful, dragging him horizontally into its phenomenally large gullet.

The heat within this animate sarcophagus and the dearth of fresh air teamed to stifle Brand-Yngar's respiration, but as soon as his sword hand found its possession he struck where he presumed the walls of his fleshy place of incarceration to be. The arch of the leviathan's throat rose beyond his reach, compelling him to stab primarily at the surface underlying his feet. Soon, though, that surface was elsewhere, for as the digestion process continued Iormungand drew him more deeply into its alimentary canal, causing him to spin and tumble. Brand-Yngar no longer essayed to right himself but only to sink Ufaellin's blade, along with those of his other weapons, into whichever part of the living conveyor belt happened to be closest at the moment.

The perforations that he made in the Midgarth Serpent's organs gave rise to fountains of blood, but in relation to the worm's total size they effected nothing more than an irritation. Furthermore, the nocent quality of the air circulating about there inside had begun taking a toll on Brand-Yngar.

He owed his remaining morale to his presupposition that (because of the practically immeasurable length of Iormungand's digestive tract) he had no shortage of time in which to cut his way to freedom, and to the Norns' failure to specify the precise form of his departure from this existence; he would postpone the afterlife for as long as he could. If only he could halt the movement carrying him farther down the serpent's insides, at least long enough to repeatedly strike the same spot, he thought might have a chance of wounding so deeply as to achieve something.

While in Grabak's haunt, Brand-Yngar had used stabs from his dagger as substitutes for holdfasts on Yggdrasil's root; he conjectured that the same tactic might immobilize him in this situation, and so he plunged the knife into flesh and braced himself by gripping the shaft with both hands. A moment later he further hardened his resistance, but, unlike the root of the World Tree, the throat encasing him was flexible; although his body no longer moved the gullet itself did, and so it still conveyed him inward. When he put even more force into fighting the flow, especially on the part of the one arm of his that would need to remain stationary while the other attacked with sword, peristalsis sundered him from his dagger. Although he tried to lunge forward so to regain possession of the knife, he quickly receded out of sight of the weapon; he knew that this specific struggle was lost and that that for his life likely was also.

Brand-Yngar responded to the catastrophe with desperate improvisation, by attempting to use his spiked shield in the same way he had the dagger. It didn't come free from his arm, to which it was strapped, but it did so from the interior surface of Iormungand's throat. He took Ufaellin and his shield, and stabbed and hacked furiously. This availed him little, but he didn't desist from the action until he ran out of strength, for in his evaluation his one true remaining hope was to enter the berserk frenzy which had multiplied his prowess before; his ire waned, though, and his feeling of resignation increased.

While he tried to recover enough muscle power and will power to resume his attack, he thought some more about his impending death. He had presumed that he would go to Valhalla, but not until now had he contemplated the specific nature of his passage into the next life. If the tales he had heard should prove true, one or more of the astral maidservants called Valkyries would come to Earth and bear his phantom up to Asgarth. Many of these winged women (whose steeds likewise had the power of flight) were known by personal names; Brand-Yngar's very favorite, whom he naturally had never seen but who he imagined to be quite beautiful, was Rota. Others, once he had established himself in the hall of heroes, would serve him victuals at every meal.

He reflected on the course of his life, and decided that he had only a pair of regrets: that he had not made Asny happy by betrothing her in a Christian ceremony, and that he had not succeeded in his endeavor to slay Iormungand. He wondered what the Norns had meant in ordaining that he would contribute to the World Serpent's downfall, since the previsioning of the future had it that not the einheriar but Thor alone would destroy the monster. Expecting to learn the answers to all his questions soon enough, he began anew his battle from within the worm.

He felt himself debilitating by degree; when he had reached a point well over one mile inside the Worm's alimentary canal, the teamed forces of intestinal heat, enzymes, and lack of oxygen had accomplished their purpose.

Brand-Yngar woke, as from sleep, to find himself mounted on a celestial horse behind a maiden mailed and armed with a spear; she had already taken him far above the world of men. From his glimpses of her visage he saw that she was indeed lovely (albeit not so appealing to him as was Asny), and thought that she might indeed be Rota, for the Valkyrie by that name was among the few who *always* appeared at scenes of war to gather slain heroes. He also discovered that his dagger, which he had not possessed at the moment of death, had somehow come home to his belt.

Too filled with wonderment to speak, he watched as Midgarth fell away and as his escort rode with him over the redoubts enclosing Asgarth. Valhalla stood in Idavoll, the central section of this world. While "Rota's" charger still coursed along with the winds over lush pastures and copses, however, a blast of music penetrated his body, along with everything else throughout the Nine Worlds; he had heard the same note when Heimdall winded his horn gently at the apex of the Rainbow Bridge, but this time its blowing signaled the onset of the Ragnarok.

They had come within sight of Valhalla, an edifice roofed with shields and spear shafts and counting 540 doors. The maid's horse yet galloped through air, but the figures now visible on the ground stood deathly still until the sound filling the macrocosm faded into silence; then, their final practice session left incomplete, the training warriors hastened to assemble into a rude sort of military formation. Somebody lacking an eye (thus looking like Othin himself, who had sacrificed one of these orbs for the sake of wisdom) issued from the palace to command them. Not long afterward, Brand-Yngar, his companion, and the pair's conveyance alighted nearby.

At the same time that the Aesir and Vanir marshaled their forces, the giants and their allies were celebrating the arrival of the time for battle. Wolf Fenris and wolf-dog Garm both burst their shackles, as did Loki. Hel sailed from her namesake land in Naglfar, the great ship she had constructed from the nails of human corpses; Hrym, the despot of the frost giants from Niflheim, acted as helmsman. Surt, his equivalent among the fire giants in the far-southern realm of Muspelheim, set out with flaming sword in hand and myriad troops at his heels. Iormungand reared up from the silt on the ocean bed and, for the first time in years, protruded his draconic head above the water level; for the first time in eternity he slithered ashore, causing destructive waves with his undulations.

These tsunamis constituted only a few of the catastrophes in Midgarth, for the world of man fully erupted into chaos. The whole earth saw bloodshed, much of it civil war. The Moon, Sun, and all other stars disappeared. Trees uprooted and mountains crumbled. The very sky tore open; through this rift came Surt and his subjects, their leader coated in magma and swirling with fire. Bifrost cracked and then disintegrated.

The opposing sides, that of the Aesir and Vanir now including Brand-Yngar, moved like metal filings attracted to a magnet. The magnet was Vigrid Field, a plain in Asgarth extending six-score leagues in each of the cardinal directions. When all the contestants had assembled, Brand-Yngar took in the sight in stupefaction; he saw arrayed there nearly all the leading personages of Norse mythology, but one conspicuous absence was that of his own idol, Thor. Hardly had he made the observation, however, before he chanced to look behind himself and noticed that the Thunderer indeed approached; marked by wild red hair and similar beard, riding in a golden chariot pulled by two magical and oversized he-goats, and clothed as always in his black-and-yellow battle garb and gear (including his belt Megingjardar, which doubled his natural strength, his war hammer Mjollnir, and his gauntlets Jarn Grieper, which enabled him to wield this famous instrument of destruction), he was unmistakable to Brand-Yngar.

Thor came not to join this particular battle, though; he merely passed by en route to his expectedly fatal clash with Iormungand. Knowing that he was watching his personal, cherished god go to his death, Brand-Yngar morbidly followed him with his gaze until the deity was no longer in sight. With no little anguish and bitterness he thought back on his own clash with the World Serpent; what had he achieved by thus sacrificing his life, if his god and the universe would perish anyway in a matter of hours?

The army of Loki, the giants, and the other monsters formed on the horizon. The ultimate battle began.

The one-eyed generalissimo knew his own specific, predestined role and those of his comrade deities in this conflict, but the rank and file of the einheriar did not; like other children, they simply followed their sire, in this case following him into combat. Their monocular leader engaged Fenris Wolf, and when Brand-Yngar and the others moved to support him versus the gargantuan, the beast's own frost-giant allies came to *its* aid. Othin did not even strike a blow at Fenris, for it opened its jaws so wide that it downed the chief of the pantheon with one gulp. Brand-Yngar, although familiar with the foretelling of this event (as well as with such a means of death), couldn't believe that he had seen the greatest of the gods lose so ignominiously; he hadn't time to think more about Othin's pathetic end, however, because one of the giants singled him out for personal engagement. Fenris was still too occupied to take action against him and his fellow einheriar, since Othin's son Vidar sought to avenge his father's demise.

The premier confrontation of Brand-Yngar's afterlife opened with a fire giant, Iarntosk, attempting to crush him with a stomp of his mighty foot. The column-like leg failed to hit its mark, but Brand-Yngar's recovery from dodging it did not come in time for him to strike back. Next, Iarntosk revealed a hammer rather like Thor's, but lacking its capability of acting like a boomerang when thrown, and far larger (even more so than a maul with a shaft of proportional mallet-length, although the giant could heave it in one hand). The fire giant slammed this bludgeon onto the turf where Brand-Yngar had stood just a moment earlier, leaving a noticeable depression. Taking care and precious seconds to career between this shallow pit and the footprint, Brand-Yngar moved to the attack; Iarntosk, however, stepped far enough backward as to be well out of sword and shield-spike range, and, again while stooping, swung his weapon to drive his tiny foe into the soil.

This time it was Brand-Yngar who backpedaled out of harm's way, for temporarily retreating at least negated the possibility of tumbling into the growing number of potholes created by the maul. Another blow meant for him impacted Vigrid Field, and then another; Iarntosk retained his so-far unfruitful strategy because he knew that by pacing much farther in reverse Brand-Yngar would become cornered against a different one-on-one battle. The fire giant struck once more; rather than move away this time, Brand-Yngar wrapped himself around the hammer's handle and held on as Iarntosk, surprised and unable to yet stem the momentum of his action, jerked his arm upward to aim the next blow. Brand-Yngar released his grip on the hammer but not on sword or shield, allowing his opponent's own strength to propel him through the air. The flight ended upon his making contact with Iarntosk's tangled and twining beard, within reach of the giant's vulnerable neck; here Brand-Yngar thrust with Ufaellin, killing the fiend almost immediately. So quickly did Iarntosk in fact fall that Brand-Yngar needed to leap for safety from his lofty place, and would have suffered injury had not the extraordinary helm and bear-hide garments saved him.

Immediately after he delivered the fatal thrust, a cry of alarm rang from elsewhere on the battlefield; it was audible through the rest of the clangor because of its harmony, although its tone spoke of discordance and grief.

Brand-Yngar looked around in order to see who would next meet him in combat, rather than who had bellowed in such cacophony, but from the source of the noise's issuance approached Iarntosk's equally monstrous brethren Dokkhild, Svartnir, Grimvidur, and Thrudsaxi. Of the four only Thrudsaxi overtly possessed weaponry, which fact Brand-Yngar found odd but attributed to the reputation of some giants for having magical skills.

As if cued by this presupposition, Dokkhild halted his bipedal movement and shifted his shape into that of an eagle larger than ten such normal birds, now winging his way to close to the attack. Grimvidur simply vanished, but the other two underwent no apparent physical change. Thrudsaxi launched his spear, which sailed well over the head of his target. Brand-Yngar couldn't believe that the throw would have missed so badly unless the giant had for whatever reason intended this, but the eagle was already swooping upon him, and so he devoted his attention to the oversized raptor. Unlike an ordinary helmet, which would have narrowed the scope of his sight, the one he wore allowed him a wide view; as he tilted his head to follow the eagle his peripheral vision captured the spear *circling* so that it aimed toward his back. Since the missile has magic, he inferred, it might very well breach his bear pelt; he crouched, hoping that the missile would strike the diving bird of prey, but each attack instead swept past one of his shoulders. The eagle-giant beat its wings to return control to its flight, and the projectile rocketed back to the hand of its owner.

Svartnir had by this time come close enough for Brand-Yngar to hurt him, and so the Northman lashed out with Ufaellin. The heretofore juggernaut of a sword thudded against Svartnir's unarmored flesh; because of the blade's excellence it did not fracture, but Brand-Yngar's hands felt the shock waves from its abject failure in penetration. The thurse, as this kind of stupid but prodigious giant was known, returned a swat with the hand for this lack of success. Battered and catapulted off his feet by the cuffing, Brand-Yngar understood why Svartnir used no weapons: thanks to his corundum-like hardness, "His whole body *is* one."

Brand-Yngar collected himself and promptly received a strike from another hand, this one not as powerful but unseen. "I needn't ask if the fourth one has joined the fight," he told himself. Taking no immediate action to defend himself, he instead used the time to switch his shield from his left arm to the position on his back, where he carried it when not expecting trouble. This, he rapidly reasoned, would protect him from rear attacks by the magic spear. Grimvidur again boxed him, knocking him nearly flat, and while he still laid on his back the giant in eagle form descended upon him with talons outstretched. Brand-Yngar unhooked his dagger from his belt and, without rising, flung the fabulous weapon skyward; it hit Dokkhild in the area of his black heart, whereupon he sputtered to the ground. Brand-Yngar scrambled out of the thurse's path with his neck crooked downward, so that his helmet's horns extended forward almost horizontally, and he changed his orientation repeatedly; this was so that no member of the remaining trio could stay to his rear for long, and so that the armature on his head would cause harm to Grimvidur if he should dare to aim for there. Had he any familiarity with Greek mythology, he would have realized that he rather gave the impression of a minotaur holding multiple opponents at bay.

Thrudsaxi seemed poised for another hurl of the spear, but forbore because Svartnir was targeting Brand-Yngar with a kick. Brand-Yngar dropped and half-rolled, half-somersaulted under the sweep of the fire giant's foot, coming up closer to Thrudsaxi. This time the spear-wielder maintained his grip on his weapon, thrusting it to a point just above and behind the cranium of Brand-Yngar, whom it then bit by actually contorting its shaft into a J-figure. His shield stopped the gleaming spearhead as planned, and before Thrudsaxi could pull the weapon back, Brand-Yngar directed Ufaellin in an overarching slice that severed the curved ash-wood with a noisome crack. His precious spear destroyed, Thrudsaxi shamefacedly fled the scene.

Svartnir caught Brand-Yngar from behind, locking one huge hand around the human's knees and another just above the waist, and then hoisted him to the level of his chest. Brand-Yngar had his arms free, but what did that avail him if the thurse who clasped him had no vulnerability even to his sword? As Svartnir turned and remained standing, like a girl carrying her doll, Brand-Yngar came to the realization that the fire giant intended to keep him defenseless versus a presumably oncoming Grimvidur.

Brand-Yngar had been struggling as a natural, practically involuntary reaction against the infrangible grip, but now it abruptly occurred to him to cease resistance with the same abruptness; Svartnir, unprepared for this instant slackening, noted with chagrin that the human had slipped through his hands. Brand-Yngar rolled as he dropped to the meadow, and upon steadying himself he saw the formation of a large, roughly oval depression in the grass a few yards away; Grimvidur evidently also had been taken by surprise, and had just then shifted his stance. Brand-Yngar lurched toward the clandestine enemy and swung Ufaellin over the evanescent footprint. The resultant shout of rage and pain, along with the crash as of a massive body to the ground, told him sans words that he had hacked through the fire-thurse's ankle.

Brand-Yngar returned his attention to Svartnir, and none too early, for the genuflecting giant aimed a thunderous hammer-blow toward him with the bottom of his fist. This impacted the turf, but not Brand-Yngar, who darted a few yards without attempting to strike back. Svartnir tried again, with the same result; he then made sweeps and kicks with his tremendous arms and legs, but always failed to wound his weaving and zigzagging adversary.

Brand-Yngar halted. Since the din of the battle had lessened somewhat (as a result of the dissolution of the two opposing hosts into many smaller, unofficial formations, and of the fact that the number of fallen and thus silent combatants had grown), he called to the fire giant, bellowing: "I cannot slay you, nor you me. I propose an arrangement, therefore, that we shall both vow to honor." Svartnir also ceased fighting, and listened.

"Is the toughness of your skin permanent, or have you control over it?"

The giant answered, "I can do without it whenever I wish."

"In that case, if you pledge to abandon this magic of yours, I swear to allow you an unobstructed strike at me—indeed, as many as you want, so long as your skin is no harder than is normal for a thurse."

Svartnir broke into a broad smile. "I agree." He nudged closer and poised his right fist directly above Brand-Yngar's head, looking like a tracklayer readying to drive in the final spike in the construction of a railway. Brand-Yngar forestalled him with a gesture, and in the ensuing pause shed his buckler, sword, and helmet; he stood up rigidly, having his chin level with the ground, his arms slack at his sides, and his crown at the meeting place of the imaginary crosshairs serving to aim the looming weapon of flesh.

Although ready, Svartnir could not act, for a godlike voice from below and behind abruptly called "thurse!" Whirling to meet the disturbance, the fire giant saw Thor's son Magni, carrying a hammer similar to, but lesser than, his sire's famous one; before Svartnir could react further, the godling slammed this weapon into and crushed one of the huge legs, sending the monster to the ground. With Svartnir thus immobilized, Magni delivered a coup-de-grace to the skull.

Brand-Yngar prostrated himself before his savior. He had seen this personification of strength advancing to the scene of combat, and had deduced from legend that his unearthly might would prevail against even the phenomenal hardness of Svartnir's skin. To prevent the fire giant from detecting the new enemy who stalked him, however, and thus perhaps attacking preemptively, Brand-Yngar had wagered that in making his proposition he could hold the thurse's attention long enough for Magni to close; he had cast off his armor and weapons in order to ensure that the god would not arrive too late to rescue him from a second death. As Brand-Yngar had suspected, the foe had behaved treacherously regarding the terms of the bargain, but this had not prevented him from being dispatched.

Magni had time to receive just a little of Brand-Yngar's adulation before moving on to fight elsewhere on the field. Brand-Yngar also had only a short respite before again joining battle, but, as Ragnarok raged, the number of living combatants decreased until, finally, hardly any could be found; the giants and gods were dying just as was their universe. Now, hours after the commencement of the climactic conflict, Brand-Yngar saw that he had no recourse other than to make his way through the corpses and try to find one of the banquet halls where, according to the tales of old, those reaching them would survive the calamity.

Merely a few such places existed, including Everfrost and Gimle. Thanks to his helmet, and to the fact that Breidalblik, or Broadview, lay in "the greenest of woods" and so contrasted sharply with the spreading envelope of desolation, Brand-Yngar espied this particular homestead in the distant area called Broad-Shining. It had belonged to Baldur, the beloved "bright god," whose murder through the machinations of Loki had commenced the Fimbulwinter and resulted in the Ragnarok. Perhaps that hall, left empty by death, would serve as a haven for life.

As he progressed toward the refuge, Brand-Yngar's feeling of relief succumbed to worry, for he had heard that no unclean thing could make an appearance in Broadview. He hadn't much confidence that he qualified morally to find harbor there, but, then, had he really any option? It had probably become too late to reach the other halls, regardless.

The gigantomachy that Brand-Yngar had left behind was over, but its effects were not; the now-dead Surt had inflamed the whole macrocosm, and the Earth was sinking into the ocean whence it had risen. Should the legends hold true, Baldur would come back to life and head a new pantheon, comprising Magni and a handful of other deities who had survived Ragnarok; better and purer than their antecedents, they would reign over a golden age that would see creation begin anew. Midgarth would be reborn from the primal chaos, and the sole surviving human couple, Life and Leifthrasir, would repopulate it with their progeny. He thought hopefully on these stories as he arrived at, and entered, Broadview.

Brand-Yngar did not need to open the door to the deserted hall. Not only did he find no divinity inside, he also seemed to have been the first being of any sort to flee there from Vigrid Field. He strolled idly about the house before his battle fatigue compelled him to sit.

He had been mentally reviewing the extraordinary events of the past several years of his life, and afterlife, when he happened to observe that company was indeed present, although he had not heard anybody enter after determining positively that the building had no other occupant. He started from his seat, but the shadowed figure made no move toward him. After a few seconds of expecting the mystery man to announce himself or at least acknowledge the Northman's presence, Brand-Yngar initiated the conversation on his own: "Who are you?"

The stranger replied out of the gloom, "I am the one who died, but has risen."

Brand-Yngar felt so physically weak, all of a sudden, that he might have collapsed even had he not chosen to lie face down as a token of submission. "O Baldur," he cried in a quivering voice; he had meant to continue, but could think of nothing else to say to a god.

The addressed at last came forward to be viewed, and said, "Lift your head, Brand-Yngar Magnusson." Brand-Yngar complied with the instruction, while keeping the rest of his body prostrated, and saw that this person did not look very much like a depiction of Baldur, or, for that matter, anyone else he had ever seen; he had a rather dark complexion and an aquiline nose, wore a robe of the purest white and a crown apparently composed of thorns, and appeared to have wounds in His wrists, feet, and side. "I am Jesus, the Christ."

Recognizing this holy Name as that of which Asny had so often spoken, Brand-Yngar wanted to say "Forgive me, Lord, for not believing in You." As before, though, no utterance proceeded from him.

Christ, knowing the mortal's thoughts, said with a smile: "Even while you did not believe in me, you worked toward my Father's ends for this world. Men may have given you a byname because of your arson, but I call you thus because when your parents had you baptized, the priest put a brand upon you, that is, marked you as mine forever.

"Nor is it by mistake that you have the name 'Yngar.' Have you not an oarsman known as Ivar inn yngri?" Brand-Yngar nodded his affirmation. "Do you, then, fail to notice the similarity between his byname and your baptismal name? 'Inn yngri' denotes 'the younger'; you have always thought of your 'Yng-' as a reference to the false god of that appellation, and, indeed, your mother and father named you after a kinsman for whom it meant just that, but I tell you now that it really identifies you with me, for I am the 'younger,' the Son.

"Society has even surnamed you correctly, because you are not the son merely of the *man* 'Magnus' but also of 'the great,' which is the Latin meaning, because omnipotent God has adopted you as one of his children." Again comprehending what went on in Brand-Yngar's mind, the Savior added, "Your myth holds that einheriar become sons of the idol 'All-Father;' this has part of the truth, since you have God the Father as your heavenly sire. It was He to whom the ravens referred when they spoke of the Father of All, and this is also why Modgud denied that you are of Thor's lineage. Likewise, you assumed that 'Coiler' and 'World Serpent,' whom you were chosen to help defeat, allude to the imaginary Iormungand; they really apply to the serpent in the Garden of Eden, Satan, who, like a dragon encircling the Earth, has dominion over the fallen human world. Men also sometimes identify him with the Leviathan, which word means 'coiled one.'"

Now you wonder how ravens could talk, if they are not the magical pair said to belong to Othin; had you read the Fourth Book of Moses or heard readings from it, you might have learned that God can even place human speech in the mouth of an ass. It is not magic, nor are any other of the wonders you have seen (or experienced, in the case of berserking), but rather the prerogative of God to make exceptions to His physical laws."

Moreover, when they instructed you to fare forth, they were simply telling you that you must put away your fears and trust in God; it had nothing to do with the delusion of 'trance traveling.' The person you took for a dis is actually your guardian angel, shielding you against malefic daemons that you call meinvaettir, and the 'valkyrie' who brought you to Heaven (your 'Asgarth') is an angel as well. You know the 'World Tree' Yggdrasil also as the 'Tree of Life,' but you have not considered that the first man and woman found a Tree of Life in their Garden."

You were wrong to want to ascertain your *destiny*, but right to seek to know your 'wyrd,' since I am the Wyrd, or Word, made flesh."

When you thought that the Midgarth Serpent killed you, you merely became dead toward sin, as St. Paul wrote that my disciples must. The sound that you interpreted as the fateful blast from Gjall came in truth from the trump of the Archangel Gabriel, and it did signal that the time had come for the ultimate battle; not the 'Doom of the Gods,' however, but Armageddon. (The title of the former is, however, appropriate, because the one true God has swept away the deities of the pagans.) Subsequently there shall be created a new Heaven and Earth, just as in the mythology that you have believed."

What you underwent is merely a preview of Armageddon, for it and my Last Judgement of the living and the dead cannot take place until those who follow me have preached the Gospel all over the world. Because of the persistent prayers of Asny have I given you all these mystical experiences, drawing on parallels between the Truth and the old beliefs, which resulted from a search for life's purpose that was honest but unguided by divine revelation; for you are a stiff-necked man, whom no one could have shown the Light otherwise. Go now back to your wife and friends, because the Year 1003 after my incarnation has come upon them, and they fear the worst concerning you. You will see that your gifts of weaponry are real, but so are the wounds you suffered in the fight versus wickedness; these befell you as partial punishment for the evil that you yourself have worked, and you will face much more adversity before your life finishes. When it does, however, provided you have continued to make war upon unrighteousness, I shall invite you to a banquet hall infinitely finer than this one. In the meantime, fret over nothing; I have overcome the world!"

With that, Christ vanished, and Brand-Yngar found himself at the edge of the Vinland forest, within sight of the strand where the Kraken lay and where Asny and the crewmen presently congregated. He ran to there, in an ecstasy he had never before known.

When his associates spotted him coming, there arose a roar of acclamation. "Captain, we had thought you dead!" one of them exclaimed.

"I have only just begun to live." Their joy turned to disbelief as he boarded and hauled down the raven flag. "We will return this ship to the King of Norway; I will nevermore be a Viking," he said in front of elated Asny, "nor shall you rogues who have sailed with me. I will be nothing *less* than a Christian, and I wager that you will also, if you hear my story. To serve God is the greatest adventure of all!"

FINIS

EPILOG

Brand-Yngar married Asny in a proper ceremony, and she bore him seven children: Hallvarth ("rock defender"), Dalla ("brightness"), Hjort ("stag"), Vestmar ("west famous"), Drifa ("driven snow"), Dag ("day"), and Hakon ("of the chosen race"). Several of the boys grew up to imitate their father in feats of arms; Hallvarth (1005–1054), for instance, the first-born, joined the Byzantine Empire's Varangian Guard. Their mother died giving birth to the last, after a happy life that lasted longer than was usual for that era. Brand-Yngar received a royal pardon upon making restitution for his crimes, and (killed in battle versus further enemies of God) left this world in 1035, after many further exploits that have passed into legend.

Printed in the United States
98012LV00004B/8/A

9 781413 763775